Sweetblood

PETE HAUTMAN

Simon Pulse
New York London Toronto Sydney

First Simon Pulse edition September 2004

SIMON PULSE
An imprint of Simon & Schuster
Children's Publishing Division
1230 Avenue of the Americas
New York, NY 10020

Also available in a Simon and Schuster Books for Young Readers hardcover edition.
Designed by Ann Sullivan
The text of this book was set in Century Schoolbook.

Manufactured in the United States of America
10

The Library of Congress has cataloged the hardcover edition as follows:
Hautman, Pete, 1952-
Sweetblood / Pete Hautman.
p. cm.
Summary: After a lifetime of being a model student, sixteen-year-old Lucy Szabo is suddenly in trouble at school, at home, with the "proto-vampires" she has met online and in person, and most of all with her uncontrolled diabetes.
ISBN 0-689-85048-4 (hc.)
[1. Diabetes—Fiction. 2. Vampires—Fiction. 3. Interpersonal relations—Fiction. 4. High schools—Fiction. 5. Schools—Fiction.] I. Title.
PZ7.H2887 Sw 2003
[Fic]—dc21 2002011179

ISBN-13: 978-0-689-87324-9 (Simon Pulse pbk.)
ISBN-10: 0-689-87324-7 (Simon Pulse pbk.)

For Mark and Amy

I would like to thank Alice Beard for her support and encouragement when I began writing *Sweetblood* a quarter of a century ago; Jennifer Flannery, David Gale, and Ellia Bisker for their understanding of, enthusiasm for, and commitment to the YA field; and Mary Logue for too many things to tally. I must also acknowledge the three pillars of modern vampire fiction: Bram Stoker, Anne Rice, and Joss Whedon. The Undead would not be walking without them.

CONTENTS

1. Blood 1
2. Friendship 6
3. Undead 12
4. Sblood 19
5. Blue Eyes 27
6. The Sad Truth About Bloodsucking Demons 35
7. Draco 44
8. Femmes Fatale 52
9. Low 63
10. *BLAH BLAH BLAH* 70
11. French Cuisine 77
12. *Poisson* 85
13. Night Creature 95
14. Espresso Yourself 103
15. Butterflies and Beer 110
16. Wine Red 121
17. Fuzz 133
18. Bad Girl 139
19. Shrink-Wrap 144
20. Studying 155
21. Adrift 162
22. Angst 170
23. Trick or Treat 182
24. Bizarro 190
25. Wine and Chocolate 198
26. Snail 213
27. Logic 218
28. Me 226
29. Blue Sky 237

1

Blood

Blood is my friend. Without it my cells shrivel. Without it I die.

At night, alone with myself, I hear it rushing through arteries and veins, platelets tumbling in a soup of plasma and glucose through slick, twisty tubes, lining up to enter narrow capillaries, delivering oxygen and fuel, seeking idle insulin. It is a low-pitched sound: wind passing through woodlands.

I hear a higher pitched sound too: A demon dentist drilling, rising and falling but never stopping. It is the sound of my thoughts.

Alone, at night, with myself, the low sound and the high sound become music. If I lie perfectly still and quiet the concert separates me from my body. Eyes closed, I float above myself, supported on a cloud of song.

But these are my secrets, things I do not talk about. You don't want people to think you're crazy, not even your best friends.

Even if you are crazy. *Especially* if you are.

When I was six years old I found a dying bat, probably *Myotis lucifugus*. Or maybe it was *Desmodus rotundus*, the infamous vampire bat, on vacation from South America. Nobody knows for sure. I saw the bat flopping around on the grass. I didn't know what it was, but being only six and fond of all small creatures, I picked it up. Its wings were velvety soft and it made squeaking, mewling protests. I put it in my pocket and took it home to show to my mother.

She let out a shriek. That was ten years ago, but I can still hear her screech echoing in my skull. I dropped the bat—*flop flop flop*—on the kitchen floor and my mother grabbed her broom and *WHACK WHACK WHACK*. She swept it into the plastic dustpan and carried it outside and dropped it in the trash. Another pet story with a sad ending.

That night when my father got home he heard the story of the bat. He did not scream like my mother but instead got very gruff and concerned and made me show him my hands. Scratches, scratches everywhere. Did it bite? He kept asking me did it bite. I was going *NO NO NO,* but my hands were scratched from picking raspberries at the Fremonts', where I was not supposed to go, and he was holding my hands too hard and he was furious and my mother was whining and I was screaming and shrieking loudest of all, I'm sure.

WHERE IS IT?

The bat is in the trash, my mother tells him. He drops my scratched hands and runs outside, but the bat is gone. The trash has been picked up. My mother and I sob in the face of my father's rage.

I don't remember much about the hospital. They say that rabies shots are painful, and that there are a lot of them. I don't remember the shots. Maybe I have blocked the memories, or maybe they have dissolved into the memories of all the other shots I've had in my life. I've had a *lot* of shots. All I remember now is that the emergency room doctor was very calm and gentle, and I liked him.

"Little girls aren't supposed to play with sick bats," he told me, smiling.

"I'm not so little," I said.

I don't know why I remember that and not the shots.

Fish, my endocrinologist, tells me that the bat and the rabies shots had nothing to do with my diabetes. I am not so sure. How can you give a six-year-old girl rabies shots and not have it affect her? The way I see it (and I have done a lot of research in this area) the rabies vaccination trains the body's immune system to attack. That's what vaccines do. They don't actually kill the bacteria or virus, they just activate the immune system. As soon as the supposed rabies virus starts to multiply, the immune system is ready and waiting and *BAM*. The virus never has a chance.

But here's the thing: That same immune system that kills rabies viruses kills other kinds of cells too. The cells that make insulin, for instance. Beta cells. I have been over this with Fish. He doubts that the rabies shots did anything bad to me. He says that my immune system destroyed my beta cells all on its own. Fish (real name: Harlan Fisher, M.D.) knows his stuff, but he still can't tell me why, three months after the rabies shots, this little girl guzzled an entire half gallon of orange juice in just one afternoon.

❧

Blood is my enemy. It carries death to my cells.

I still remember gulping orange juice right out of the carton, cold and sweet, pouring down my throat. Six years old, I could hardly lift the carton, but I was so desperately thirsty—*gulp gulp gulp*—I could've won a guzzling contest. Also, I could've won a peeing contest, because everything I drank went straight into the toilet.

You'd think my mother would've noticed earlier, but it didn't hit her how sick I was until I'd gone through about six cartons of juice in one week—and wet my bed twice. Then it was *whoosh*—off to the doctor. Dr. Gingrass with the big mole on his giant nose. He's the one who gave me my first shot of insulin. I stared numbly as he mixed the cloudy insulin with the clear, had me lift my shirt, and pinched up a bit of baby fat and slipped the needle in. It didn't hurt a bit, but my mother was freaking, crying and asking the poor doctor how this could happen. Even then, I knew enough to be embarrassed by her, but it wasn't until years later that I came to understand the fullness of what had happened to me. Insulin is more than just a treatment for the disease called *diabetes mellitus*. It is the thin strand that holds me to earth.

Without it I die.

2

Friendship

I've had three or four best friends in my life. They don't last. We have a fight, or they just get sick of my weirdness, and all of a sudden we aren't friends anymore. Or they go away. My previous best friend, Kathy Wasserman, moved away to St. Louis. That was a year ago. We e-mailed each other a few times, but it just wasn't the same. I haven't heard from her in months.

Right now I don't have a real best friend, but if I had to pick one it would be Mark Murphy, who lives down the block and across the street and who is one of the few people at school who doesn't treat me like a freak. He calls me Skeeter. He has called me that since he moved into the neighborhood nine years ago. That was after the bat thing, after I got sick. I don't know why he started calling me Skeeter. Nobody else ever did. Little kids are sensitive that way. Maybe he knew that one day I would turn into a bloodsucking fiend, a human mosquito.

It is Sunday, day of rest for some people. I put on my black makeup and my purple lipstick and my black leather jacket and black leggings and my lace-up motorcycle boots and my sunglasses so dark I can hardly see through them and I go out to sit in the shade on the front steps to read Anne Rice and disturb the churchgoing neighbors by my mere existence. I am only pretending to read, though. Mostly I am imagining moving out of my parents' house and into an apartment over by the college and hanging out in coffeehouses and taking writing classes and meeting people who don't know anything at all about me. I don't smoke, but when I imagine myself independent and on my own I always see myself smoking nonfilter cigarettes and drinking straight espresso from a small, cracked cup.

I am thinking about this as Mark Murphy comes strolling by, dragging his size-thirteen Nikes, hands buried deep in his jeans pockets. He is wearing a faded orange Seward Stingers sweatshirt and a baseball cap with the name of a tractor company stitched on the front. Mark is not into fashion.

"Hey, Skeeter," he says, stopping on the sidewalk.

I lower my book, giving my mouth an irritated twist to make him think he has interrupted a really good part.

"What're you reading?" he asks.

I hold up the book. He comes closer so that he can see the cover: *The Queen of the Damned.*

"What's it about?" he asks.

"Vampires."

"Vampires suck." He laughs so that I will know he is making a joke.

I try not to smile, but I can't help it. Mark always knows how to make me laugh.

I say, "Got a cigarette, Monkey Boy?" I gave him that nickname a few summers ago when he fell out of a tree and broke his arm. It was also to get back at him for always calling me Skeeter. Which, actually, I like.

"Sorry. I didn't think you smoked."

"I don't, but I'm thinking of taking it up. Don't ask me why."

"Why?"

"Told you not to ask me that."

"I mean why can't I ask you that?"

"You just did. Actually, since you insist on knowing every detail of my life, I'll tell you. I think it would be fulfilling to have a habit. Something self-destructive to do on a daily basis."

"Why cigarettes? Why not just start smoking crack?"

"Too expensive."

"How about heroin? You're not scared of needles."

"Ha-ha."

"Hey, you going to that thing tonight?"

"What thing?"

"You know."

I stare at his face. When Mark was a little kid he had a broad, friendly face: brown eyes and freckles and a huge grin that made his teeth look small—a face that made old ladies want to pinch his cheeks. Then, a few years ago, he started growing like crazy and everything got out of whack. His face stretched out from top to bottom, his permanent teeth came in big and crowded, and his eyes got closer together. I can still see the little kid he used to be, but it takes some effort. He still has most of his freckles. I can also see another Mark—the good-looking man he will one day become.

"You mean the block party," I say.

Mark nods.

"I don't think I *do* block parties," I say.

"Two words." He holds up two fingers, the sign for peace—or victory. "Free food."

I laugh. Mark loves to eat more than anything.

"Besides," he says, "What else are you gonna do on a Sunday night?"

"You mean besides eat burnt bratwurst and high-risk potato salad with a bunch of little kids and half-drunk parental types? Gee, I don't know . . . maybe beat myself over the head with a baseball bat?"

"Yeah, right. Well, *I'm* going."

"You have a good time." I return my attention to Anne Rice.

Mark stands there for a few seconds, then says, "You know, Lucy, I liked you a lot better before you got all punk."

"I'm not punk."

"Well, *goth* then."

"I'm not *goth.*"

"Well, you're *something.*" He lets that one hang for a beat, then shuffles off.

My best friend.

I experience mixed feelings, but I'm used to that. One of my feelings is regret that I might have hurt *his* feelings. I also feel irritation that he judged me, relief that he's gone, disappointment that he has left, and delight that he actually thinks I'm *something.*

On the wall next to my bed I have written some lines from a poem by Walt Whitman:

> Do I contradict myself?
> Very well then I contradict myself.
> (I am large, I contain multitudes)

3

Undead

I am not cool. Dead people are cool.

I am not dead. I am Undead.

Had I been born a hundred years ago I would be very cool. I would be cold. Cold bones and shreds of gristle moldering deep beneath a crumbling headstone.

People worry about race relations—blacks and whites and Asians and Aborigines and so forth—but I think that there are only two races that matter: the Living and the Undead. These races have been created by modern medicine, and with every year that passes, the numbers of the Undead grow. It is inevitable.

My mother is among the Living. My father is Undead. He had an emergency appendectomy a few years ago. Saved by modern medicine, like me.

The Chinese have a saying: If you save a man's life, you are responsible for him. In other words, by saving someone's life, you have inflicted that person's continued existence upon the world. Whatever he does from then on—be it good or evil—it's your responsibility. So who is responsible for me?

I ask my mother what's for dinner.

"Dinner?" Her brow scrunches up as though I've asked her the atomic weight of cesium.

"Yeah. You know. Food? Like we eat every night?"

She says, "Honey, tonight's the block party!" My mother always calls me Honey or Sweetie or Sugar. I think it's a subconscious effort to undo my diabetes. It's moments like these that make me wonder what cabbage leaf she found me under.

"Oh. I guess I can make myself a cheese sandwich."

"Aren't you feeling well, Sweetie?" She reaches out a hand as if to feel my forehead. I step back.

"I'm fine," I say. I know exactly what she's going to say next, and she says it.

"Do you need a snack?" My mother is deathly afraid of my insulin reactions. (Fish prefers to call them *hypoglycemic episodes*.)

"No, I do not need a snack. If I needed a snack I would eat something. I just don't feel like eating bratwurst for dinner."

"I'm bringing vegetarian beans, Honey. Your favorite."

"I have to write a paper," I say.

"Oh!" That one throws her.

"I've got a fifteen-hundred-word essay due tomorrow."

"Oh! That sounds like quite a project. How many pages is that?"

"A lot." Actually, the paper was due a week ago, but I haven't been paying much attention to due dates lately, which is probably why I'm flunking two classes. The school has been sending my parents letters, so it's going to be hard for her to tell me I can't skip the block party to do schoolwork.

"I guess we could leave you some beans," she says.

I give her my most syrupy-sweet, lovey-dovey, up-yours smile. "Gee, thanks, Mom."

I have about six or seven insulin reactions every week. Mostly they are no big deal—I get shaky and start to sweat and I quick cram something sweet in my mouth and a few minutes later everything's cool. But sometimes I get cranky and don't know my blood sugar's gone out of whack, and I throw a fit over, say, not being able to find a sock. I'm sort of unpredictable and nasty when my blood glucose gets low, which partly explains why my mother gets nervous around me.

The other reason she gets nervous is because there have been a few times when I lose it completely. One time she came home and all of the kitchen cupboards had been emptied onto the floor and I was lying unconscious on top of a pile of breakfast cereals and crackers and canned tuna fish. She had to call 911. I woke up to find Fish bending over me looking straight into my eyeball with a flashlight.

"Couldn't decide what to eat?" he said.

"Nothing looked good to me."

He laughed. Fish understands. He's had diabetes since he was nineteen. He's Undead too.

A few weeks ago in art class we had to paint self-portraits. I painted a picture of a glowing blond girl with rosy cheeks and a huge toothy smile and big blank pale gray eyes.

Mrs. Winter looked at it and said in her wintry voice, "Perhaps I wasn't clear on the self-portrait concept, Lucy."

"Really?" All innocent, blinking honey-colored eyes.

"One would think that you would be able to approximate the hair color, at least. I would say yours is quite black." She turned away. I opened a fresh jar of black tempera paint and began to follow her instructions.

What I didn't tell her, because it was none of her business, was that the picture I had painted was as honest a self-portrait as I could make. It was the Lucy I saw when I looked into a mirror. Blond and stupid and grinning and thoughtless and—you could see it in the eyes—blind as the bat that bit me. Or didn't bite me. Whatever.

The hair was my real hair color. I've been dyeing it black since the eighth grade, but Mrs. Winter didn't know that. And she'd never seen me smile, so she didn't recognize the teeth. And she didn't know anything at all about diabetes and retinopathy, and how kids that get diabetes when they are six years old can go blind—something I think about a lot.

Fish says that's not true. It used to be true, but my generation is smarter, he says. He says if I control my blood sugar I can live to be 100 and have dozens of kids and fly to the moon for vacations. "When I was a kid," he says, "they told me I'd never make it through medical school."

I used the whole jar of black paint, laying it on so thick that the cardboard got all wavy. I would have painted her *all* black, but my name is Lucy, short for Lucinda, which means light, so I left the whites of her eyes and her two canine teeth.

Mrs. Winter gave me a D.

When my dad gets home from the golf course he knocks on my door, waits a few seconds, then sticks his head in. His face is red from the sun, but his hairless dome is white. He is smiling. Dad is in sales, and when you are in sales you have to smile all the time. I think that's why he is always so tired.

"Hey, Kiddo." He always calls me Kiddo or Tiger or Sport. This is not as bad as Sweetie, Sugar, or Honey. In fact, I actually like it—unless he does it in public.

"Hi," I say. I am sprawled the wrong way on my unmade bed with my nose in Anne Rice's book. "How'd you do?" He likes me to ask about his game.

"Shot a seventy-eight!" He is proud of his score.

"That's great, Dad."

His head looks around my room. I imagine it as disembodied, just a head that drifted home from Longview Country Club. His eyes take in the piles of dirty clothing, mostly black, and my rubber bat hanging from the ceiling, suspended by a thread. He looks at my self-portrait hanging blackly on the wall above me and his smile loses a few watts.

"You are one spooky kid," he says.

"I do my best." I can't quite suppress a grin.

He picks up on it and his own smile returns to full luminescence. He winks at me. I wink back. He taught me to wink when I was about six years old. It's a thing we do.

"You coming to the block party?" he asks.

"No."

His eyebrows go up. When my mother is perplexed or concerned or whatever, her eyebrows scrunch together, but Dad's go straight up like two levitating caterpillars.

"Why not?" he asks, as if he can't imagine how any sane person could pass up bratwurst and Jell-O mold.

"I'm not feeling so good," I say. "I got my period."

"Oh!" His mouth closes and he gets his serious look. "Well, okay then, Sport." His head withdraws. I laugh silently. All I have to do is mention menstruation and he panics. Like most guys, my father is scared to death of a little blood.

4

Sblood

The Queen of the Damned is not as lame as most vampire books, but it's typically inaccurate. She gives vampires all these superpowers, and if they don't get blood they starve, and sunlight kills them. I happen to know that none of that is true.

Ignorant people always fall back on the supernatural to explain things. Like when a baby girl has a deadly disease and for some reason she survives they say, "It's a miracle! God saved her!" Or the baby dies and they say, "God took her."

It's the same thing with vampires. Many years ago, ordinary people saw some behavior that frightened and confused them. But instead of trying to figure it out, they made the poor, wretched creatures into evil monsters with mysterious powers.

I have read almost everything ever written about vampires. You might say that I am an expert. Real vampires do not turn into bats. They don't have fangs or superpowers, and they are not immortal. The truth is, the Age of the Vampire ended back in the 1920s, when a man named Sir Frederick Banting extracted a few milliliters of insulin from a vat full of cow pancreases and injected it into a dying would-be vampire named Leonard Thompson.

Of course, there are still a lot of us *potential* vampires around.

Another knock on the door.

This time my mother's disembodied head appears. She wants to make sure I know she's left a bowl of vegetarian baked beans in the fridge. She calls them *vegetarian* baked beans so that I won't overlook the fact that she has made them special for me.

"Thanks, Mom," I say.

"Are you working on your paper?" she asks.

I've already forgotten all about the paper I'm supposed to be writing. I hold up *The Queen of the Damned*. "Research. Myth, legend, and idiocy in the twentieth century."

Her head bobs weakly and she is gone.

⁂

Before eating, I check my blood sugar like a good little diabetic. I jab my thumb with my spring-loaded finger-pricker and squeeze out a dark ruby pearl of blood. I touch the blood droplet to the sensor strip on my meter, then wait a few seconds for the machine to make its pronouncement. *Tick tick tick* . . . a number appears on the display: 234. Too high! Bad girl! Bad, bad, evil, wicked girl! Sugarcoated blood cells are destroying my body from within. Kidney failure, blindness, neuropathy, horrors!

Ho-hum. I shoot up ten units of insulin and eat the bowl of beans. Good beans, Mom, but they could be a little sweeter.

I can hear the shouts of kids down the block. When I was a little kid I loved the block parties except for the part where my mother the food cop showed me all the things I couldn't eat. No Jell-O, no brownies, no lemonade, no fruit salad. Beans and brats. That was it. According to the food police, sugar was as dangerous as heroin and arsenic combined. Now, of course, she's more enlightened. We Undead can eat like ordinary people as long as we add enough insulin to the system, but my mom still gets that panicky look whenever she sees me eating a cookie.

The thing about nondiabetics is that no matter how many times you explain the whole blood glucose/insulin/food thing to them, they just don't get it. First off, they think that because it comes down to the numbers and equations, you ought to be able to control it. Well, I *can* control it—the same way you can control how many potato chips you eat, or your temper, or a six-month-old puppy. Sometimes there's just not much you can do.

I take three or four or five shots a day. Every morning I take a dose of long-acting insulin. That's the background insulin that lasts all day. Then, whenever I eat, I take a few units of fast-acting insulin, depending on how many grams of carbohydrate I'm about to consume. Sounds simple, but there's hardly a week when I don't mess up. Any little thing can throw off the numbers—stress, hormones, exercise, illness, you name it.

I eat my beans and wonder which way my blood glucose is going. If I took too much insulin it will be dropping into the danger zone, below seventy milligrams per deciliter. I could be heading for another insulin reaction—*MEEP MEEP MEEP*—danger, Lucy Szabo, danger! Brain cells shutting down, dangerous coma ahead—*MEEP MEEP*

MEEP—get out the glucagon, doc, she's going veg-o-matic.

Or maybe I didn't take enough insulin and the beans are driving my sugars up, up and away—*400 . . . 500 . . . 800!* Uh-oh, the Big Scary: diabetic ketoacidosis. Blood going toxic, get her to emergency before she mutates into a bloodsucking fiend . . .

I eat my beans and let the numbers take care of themselves.

The Transylvania room is a place in cyberspace where so-called vampires gather. I log on as Sblood, which is short for Sweetblood, my cyberself. It's a little early—the best vampire chats happen around midnight—but Vlad714 and 2Tooth are in the chat room. I'm in a pissy mood, so I start right out complaining:

Sblood: ok you guys I'm reading The Queen of the Damned and so far it sucks. which one of you losers told me to read it?

2Tooth: Whome? JACK DOWN, blood

Sblood: stop SHOUTING.

2Tooth: Sorry.

Sblood: book is ok except for being 100% bs.

2Tooth: Mayb e90

Vlad714: *Interview* ws btr.

2Tooth: More sexy :)=

Vlad714: Y

Sblood: you guys drain any virgins lately?

Vlad714: y. virgie burger. BTW, any-body rd *the blood countess*?

2Tooth: N

Vlad714: about Elizabeth Bathory. She usedto drain the blood from virgin girls and shower in it. Truefaq.

2Tooth: HOw come she did that?

Vlad714: forever young + beuaty.

2Tooth: Sounds sticky. It work?

Vlad714: IDK

2Tooth: She drink it too?

Vlad714: IDK not done w book.

2Tooth: Wonder if she's stillarround

Sblood: that was 400 years ago, you morons. she was locked up in her castle till she died.

2Tooth: How come U know this?

Sblood: I am very well red. ;)=

Elizabeth Bathory was a pitiful psychotic monster who lived in Hungary back in the sixteenth century, right around the time of Vlad the Impaler, another pitiful psychotic monster. They both killed a lot of people, but at least old Vlad had a political agenda—he was no worse than Stalin or Hitler or Osama bin Laden. Elizabeth did her killing and dying out of vanity.

I don't know why I bother with the Transylvania room. Most of the people there are basically ignorant. Plus, they can't type. But every now and then this guy Draco pops in, and he's got some interesting perspectives on the whole vampire thing. For instance, he claims to actually be one, and

I'm not 100 percent sure he's kidding.

You meet a lot of weirdos on the net.

The chat room gets me thinking about another one of my theories. I go back to my computer and read over some old notes. All of a sudden I am writing. I write for an hour straight, my fingers hammering the keyboard. Mrs. Graham might just get her stupid essay after all. I imagine her mouth turning down as she reads.

I'll show her disturbed.

5

Blue Eyes

I am Sweetblood. I am Honey, Sweetie, and Sugar. I am Sport and Tiger and Kiddo and Skeeter. It all depends on who you are. Fish calls me Lucinda Szabo. At school they call me Lucy, or Luce.

There are 246 kids in my class and two of us are diabetic: me and Sandy Steiner. Sandy just got diabetes last year and to talk to her you'd think that God reached down and gave it to her as a gift. She was insufferably cheerful and disciplined and friendly before she got sick, but instead of calming her down, the diabetes made her even more unbearable. Now she's like the diabetes ambassador, telling anybody who will listen all about her diet and her blood sugars and how well-controlled she is. But the worst thing is that she's decided that we're the diabetes sisters. Every day she hunts me down.

This morning I almost make it to my first hour class before she finds me.

"Hey, Luce!" As usual, she looks as perfect and stiff as a store mannequin.

"Hi, Sandy."

"So how was your weekend?"

I keep on walking. "Okay."

"How have your blood sugars been?" Sandy has these perfect Julia Roberts lips that curve up when she smiles.

"I'm still alive," I say.

"Ha ha ha." Sandy laughs as if she's reading it from a script. I get very uncomfortable around her. She says, "I stayed between eighty and one forty the whole weekend. Isn't that great?"

"That's amazing," I say, both irritated and impressed. Eighty and one forty? I haven't stayed between 80 and 140 for more than a few hours *ever*. "I always get up at three in the morning to test. I'm seeing Dr. Fisher next week and he wants my diary to be complete. You know. For my pump?"

Sandy's latest thing is she wants to get an insulin pump. I think it's ridiculous. I've been controlling my diabetes for ten years with injections. You get used to it. Personally,

I don't want a machine hooked up to me twenty-fours hours a day, even one as small as an insulin pump. But Sandy is totally into her diabetes. It's her holy crusade. If the technology exists, she has to have it.

"Maybe that's not such a good idea," I say.

"What do you *mean*?" All worried.

"If Fish thinks your sugars are *too* good, he won't put you on the pump."

"What do you mean?" *Really* worried now.

"Usually they only prescribe pumps for people who can't control their diabetes."

"What? That's not *true*." She's not sure if I'm kidding her.

"Sure it is. If your control is good, they'll just keep you on the shots." We have reached room 230, my chemistry class. "See you!" I leave her standing in the hall with her perfect mouth hanging open.

Chemistry and French are my worst subjects. I am failing both so far this semester. I'm failing chemistry worst of all. Mr. BoreAss (he spells it *Boris*) is writing gibberish on the board and I am drawing pictures of red blood cells in my notebook. The red blood cell has an interesting shape, sort of like a cough drop that's been sucked on for about ten minutes, or a Life Saver with the middle filled in.

So I'm drawing and listening to BoreAss babble on about acids and bases. I don't know why I signed up for this class. Maybe because last year I was smart, but that was last year. People change.

This year my best classes are English and art, although lately I haven't been doing so good in art. Not since my black painting. Maybe I'll do a painting of red blood cells. A cutaway view of an artery with all the blood parts in full gory glory. I could do a series of paintings detailing my personal blood history, from the first bat-borne microbes to the rabies vaccination to the full-blown attack on my beta cells by my berserker immune system.

It would be an epic tragedy, a real tear-jerker.

The real tragedy this semester is that French comes right after chemistry. Most days I arrive nearly comatose.

I fell way behind in French just two weeks into the semester. *Comprendez?* Not *moi*, not hardly a word, and this is French *deux*. Mme. D'Ormay has us reading Baudelaire while I'm still trying to figure out the difference between *nuit* and *noir*.

One means black and one means night and I just can't keep them straight. Oh well. If I'm flunking one class, I might as well fail *deux*.

I enter the language lab in my usual impervious-to-learning trance but wake up when I notice a new body at the other end of the table. His hair is as black as mine, his face is pale and smooth, and he is wearing a black leather vest. Just as my eyes lock on to him, his head snaps around and he nails me with a pair of bright blue eyes.

Part of me is thinking, This is so stupid. But another part of me is *dissolving*. We stare at each other for, I don't know, two or three seconds. Inside I am *screaming* at myself to look away, but he looks away first and I feel an instant hollowness, as if he has yanked a stake from my heart.

During the next hour I do not learn much French, but I find out that Blue Eyes has just transferred here from Kennedy High on the west side of the city. Mme. D'Ormay gives him the French name Guy, pronounced "gee," as in *geek*. His real name is Dylan Redfield. Both names suit him, I think.

I used to eat lunch with some of the more disturbed kids from art class, but a couple of them ruined my appetite building tabletop sculptures out of bread and lasagna, so now I dine alone. Our school has an open campus policy, so most of the kids—the ones with jobs or money, anyway—head out to one of the nearby rude-food outlets. The rest of us either eat in the cafeteria or, when the weather's nice, out on the lawn. Today it's raining and cold, so I'm stuck sitting at my corner table in the cafeteria with my yogurt and carrot sticks and a box of blood (what I call cranberry juice in a box).

"Hey."

I look up; it's Blue Eyes.

"Hey." I try not to sound hysterical.

He puts his tray down across from me, not asking my permission.

"You're in that French class, right?" he asks.

"Oui."

He laughs as if I've said something delightful, so I forgive him for interrupting my *dejeuner*.

"I'm Dylan," he says.

"Lucy," I say, pointing at my nose with a carrot stick.

"I thought it was *Lucinda*." He makes a stab at the French pronunciation and garbles it so bad I actually giggle—and I am not the giggling type. But instead of getting offended he laughs with me, then says, "My French sucks."

"I think French sucks, period," I say. I look at his tray. He has the Seward High cafeteria special: unidentifiable glop in assorted colors, a couple of bread-and-butter sandwiches, and a carton of milk. "You gonna *eat* that?" I say. Right away I wish I hadn't, because it really isn't very nice to slam somebody's food before they eat it. I jam a carrot stick in my mouth to shut myself up.

But Blue Eyes is oblivious. He thinks I'm encouraging him to chow down, and that's what he does. I don't know what I expected, but it's a bit of a disappointment to find out that he eats like a normal teenage boy. I try not to watch as he shovels.

"So how come you sit all by yourself?" he asks abruptly.

I shrug. I'm not ready for that question.

"Are you new here, too?" He isn't going to let it go.

"I have an incurable, highly contagious disease," I tell him. It's true, except for the contagious part.

"Really? What is it? Bubonic plague?"

"Worse."

"AIDS?"

"Much worse."

He has to think hard now. "I know. Leprosy!"

"Do I look like a leper?"

"Well, I can't see *all* of you." He grins. I spend a couple seconds trying to decide whether his remark constitutes sexual harassment. I decide to let it pass.

"You don't want to know what I have," I say.

"Really?" Now he is trying to figure out if I am serious.

I'm trying to figure that one out myself. I feel as though I'm teetering on the edge of a cliff. Do I want to expose this blue-eyed *Guy* to all my unadulterated weirdness in the first five minutes of our acquaintance? Do I want to sit alone with my brown-bagged haute cuisine for the rest of the school year?

I suck my cranberry juice-in-a-box dry.

"Fact is, *Guy*," I say in my most serious whisper, "I'm a vampire."

6

The Sad Truth About Bloodsucking Demons

by Lucy Szabo

Creative Writing, 4th Period

There are many tales about vampires, but almost none of them are true. So why are there so many books about vampires? Why do so many different cultures have their own vampire stories?

The truth is, vampire legends are based upon actual fact. Vampires were (and are) real, as I shall prove in the following paper.

Most of the modern ideas about vampires come from a book by Bram Stoker titled Dracula. Count Dracula (according to the book) was a vampire who lived in a castle in Transylvania and drank blood to stay alive. He could turn into a bat, and he was hundreds of years old. He was superfast and superstrong and 100% evil. Bram Stoker got many of his ideas from Romanian folk legends, and from reading about a real historical person named Vlad Dracula, also known as Vlad the Impaler. Impalement is an interesting punishment that was quite popular in the Middle Ages. The way you do it is you insert a sharpened pole into a person's rear end and then stand the pole upright so that he squirms on top of it like a living shish kebab. This was Vlad Dracula's favorite way to punish his enemies. It was said to be very painful.

But the real Vlad Dracula was not a real vampire (as far as we know). He was just a sadistic sicko, much like Elizabeth Bathory, who liked to bathe in blood collected by murdering local maidens. She also liked to bite them and torture them.

Basically, Bram Stoker was just a writer who cobbled together a few folktales and some twisted history into a kind of ghost story. But ever since, the vampire legend has grown to become a huge force in modern literature. The true story, however, was lost in the mists of time—until now.

Most myths and legends are based on

real events. For instance, the story of Noah's Ark might have been inspired by a real flood, and the Abominable Snowman is probably a rare species of bear.

This is also true of vampires.

First, you have to realize that when the vampire stories got started there was very little knowledge about diseases and medicine. People treated cancer with leeches and rubbed dirt into cuts to make them heal. Ignorance was even greater then than it is today.

Even thousand of years ago there was some knowledge of diabetes. Not that they could do anything about it, but the ancient Greeks knew that diabetics had too much sugar in them and that no matter how much they ate, they would soon waste away to nothing. But that was all they knew.

As an insulin-dependent diabetic myself, I have read a great deal about the disease. Today, we diabetics take insulin and test our blood glucose (sugar), and most of us do okay. We worry about blindness and kidney disease and heart disease and neuropathy (terminal numbness), but that's only after many years of having the disease. But before insulin was discovered, things didn't go so good for diabetics. Without insulin to turn glucose into energy, the body's cells literally starved to death. The untreated diabetic would get hungry and thirsty, but the more they ate, the sicker they got. The sugars would build up in their blood until they were so sweet that their body would start burning up fat and muscle and eventually there would be nothing left. But it wouldn't happen right away. An untreated diabetic might take weeks or months to die, and her body might go through some very peculiar changes on its journey from life to death.

Untreated insulin-dependent diabetes is pretty much extinct today. When a person starts getting thirsty and ravenous and feeling sick and peeing all the time, they go to a doctor. The doctor gives them some insulin and a syringe and modern medicine triumphs again. So it's hard for us to imagine what it was like before, when diabetes was as incurable and fatal as the electric chair. So I have made a list of some of the symptoms of advanced, untreated diabetes. This is what might have happened to a diabetic teenage girl in the Middle Ages.

The first thing is, she starts getting very hungry and thirsty. She can't get enough water. She devours bowl after bowl of gruel (whatever that is). At first, her parents are angry at her because they are poor and gruel is not free. But she can't stop herself from eating everything in sight. Soon, she starts losing weight. She is eating like a pig, but the food is going right through her. Her parents are afraid she might be possessed. They hide her from the neighbors because if word gets out, their daughter could be burned at the stake.

Weeks go by. The girl has lost a quarter of her body weight. She is pale and she smells sweet, like honey. She sleeps most of the day, but it is a restless sleep, tossing and turning and whimpering. When she awakens she is hungry and thirsty.

She wets the bed repeatedly, and after a week of that her mother stops bringing her fresh straw and simply lets the girl lie in her own filth. The girl doesn't seem to care. She talks to herself in her sleep, crazy garbled conversations with imaginary people. Her skin becomes pale and beaded with sweat, her lips are ruby red, and she has a peculiar, acrid odor.

One day the mother brings the girl a chicken leg. The girl sits up on her soiled straw pallet and snatches the chicken leg and tears into it with the ferocity of a starved wolf. The mother recoils from what she sees—the girl's teeth have grown longer, and her mouth is bloody. She gobbles down the chicken leg, crunching the bone between her long, bloody teeth. Her breath reeks like a stew of rotten fruit and fetid meat; her eyes are so dilated that they look like black holes in reality. The mother, terrified, flees.

The next day, the girl staggers out of the cottage, looking for food. As the mid-day sun strikes her she screams and covers her eyes and crumples to the ground. Her parents are shocked to see her this way, in full sunlight. Her skin is white as a fish's belly, her hair has fallen out in patches, her limbs are thin as broom handles. The father carries his wasted daughter back to her pallet and lays her down.

The next morning the girl is still and unresponsive. Her forehead is icy cold. There is no sign of life. The mother tells the father that the girl is dead. They cover her with a sheet. They tell the neighbors that their daughter has died. Tomorrow they will bury her in the graveyard by the village church.

But that night a strange thing happens. The girl awakens. She throws aside the sheet and climbs to her feet. She does not know where she is, but she is ravenous. She staggers through the cottage, confused and terrified. The mother sees her and screams in horror. The girl claps her hands to her ears. Too loud! The terrified father grabs a knife and waves it at her. She runs from the cottage, runs from the screaming and the flashing blade. She sees a flickering light in the distance. She hears voices. She smells cooking! She heads for the light, bursts into her neighbors' cottage, grabs a chunk of pork from their stewpot and crams it whole into her mouth. The neighbors run away and the girl gobbles their supper. She wanders off into the countryside. The next day some village boys find her lying motionless in a beet field. The village elders are called. The local tooth-puller pronounces her dead; the priest says that she is possessed. They decide to burn her quickly. A pyre is erected on a hilltop. The girl's body is placed atop the enormous pile of dry logs and branches. The priest throws a torch onto the pyre and within a few seconds the flames are roaring and the villagers' faces are orange with reflected firelight. Then something inside the tower of flame moves, and they see the shape of the girl. She erupts screaming from the pyre into their midst, her entire body on fire. She twists and turns and leaps in a dance of death as the villagers run shrieking. Then she dies—for real, this time.

That is what might have happened to a diabetic a few hundred years ago. Imagine the stories the peasants would tell! All of the symptoms I described are possible symptoms of untreated diabetes. The sweet smell of too much glucose in the blood, the strange, acrid reek of advanced ketoacidosis, the rotten smell of bacterial infection. Madness, ravenous hunger, extreme sensitivity to sunlight and sound, bleeding, receding gums (that make her teeth look longer), cold, clammy skin, and deathlike coma—all resulting from untreated diabetes. Even the spontaneous, repeated revival from a deathlike coma is possible.

It seems clear to me that diabetes in the Middle Ages led to the folktales that led to Bram Stoker's book that led to Anne Rice's novels and *Buffy the Vampire Slayer* and all the other vampire stuff. Diabetics were the original, the *real* vampires. They weren't evil or superpowerful or immortal. They were just sick. Like me.

I'm actually a proto-vampire. When I take an insulin shot now, I think of it as vampire vaccine. If I quit taking insulin altogether I would become that starving vampire girl from the Middle Ages. I might come crashing into your house and eat *your* pork stew.

Or whatever.

You never know what a vampire might do to you.

1655 words (including these)

7

Draco

I get a sick feeling as soon as I turn in my paper to Mrs. Graham. Like maybe I should have left out the part about impalement, or the part where I threaten to break into her house. Oh well, I just wrote what I was thinking. She'll have to deal with it, just like I have to deal with her. I don't know why all my teachers are so hard on me. It's not like there aren't a lot of other kids doing worse in school. Buttface, the school counselor, says they're hard on me because I've got so much potential. Like because I got straight As for a couple years, all of a sudden it's not okay for me to be average. What's so terrible about slacking off for a year or two? Don't I ever get to relax?

Buttface says it'll matter when I try to get into college. Just to piss her off, I once told her I was planning to go to beautician school to learn to do manicures. Buttface sat back and stroked her glass-bead necklace. She always goes for that necklace when she gets upset. When I'm in her office she's usually pawing at it within seconds.

Buttface's real name is Ms. Butkus. She is married to a man named Steele but kept her maiden name. This reveals something about her, but I don't know what. She's not actually stupid.

After creative writing, I materialize in the doorway to her office. She is sitting behind her desk doing nothing, as if she has been waiting for me.

"Hi," I say. "It's me." Like she can't figure that out herself.

"Lucy." She smiles sleepily. Buttface's style is to stay calm under all circumstances. I think she takes tranquilizers. With her round face and heavy eyelids she looks like a little kid ready for her nappy. "How are you doing today?" Her standard question.

I shrug—my standard answer. She nods as if I have said something, so I do. "This is a preemptive visit," I say.

"Oh?"

"Yeah. You know—like for a problem that

isn't a problem yet, but you might be hearing something about it."

"Something you haven't done yet?"

"Not exactly. More like something I already did, but it hasn't hit the fan yet."

"Oh." She's still smiling, but she looks a little sad.

"I wrote this paper for Mrs. Graham. We were supposed to write an essay? It was supposed to be about our future, you know? Like, what I think my life will be like when I become a lawyer, or president, or something. Except I wrote something different."

She holds her sad smile, waiting for more.

"Anyway, in case Graham blows a blood vessel or something, I just wanted you to know."

"Know what?"

"That I was just messing around. I'm not crazy."

"Nobody thinks you're crazy."

"Yeah, right."

That night at midnight I log on and drop into Transylvania. 2Tooth and Fangs are arguing about how much blood a full-blown vampire needs to stay healthy.

Fangs666: it's the essence that s

important. Vamps eat reglar food 2. They just need a little bit ofblood ever yday

2Tooth: REEL vampires need LOTS of blood

Fangs666: depends on what U call LOTS. Maybe 1 rat worth

2Tooth: More like a pig worth

Fangs666: U know how much blood in pig?

2Tooth: DEpens on how big the pig.

Sblood: HEY. I keep telling you morons that REAL vampires died out in the 20th century.

Fangs666: blood, U don 't knw crap

Sblood: at least I know how to type. you morons know less than that.

Draco: Children, behave yourselves!

Nobody writes anything for almost a minute. We haven't heard from Draco in weeks. There is something about his "voice" that scares me.

Draco: To answer your questions, young ones, a 30 kilo Vietnamese pot-bellied pig holds 2 liters of ruby nectar. This is enough to sustain an adult Overman for 2 weeks, more or less, depending upon his level of activity. That is about 150 milliliters per day. Of course, we eat other things as well, such as the rest of the pig.

Fangs666: what if you can't get it?

Draco: not get blood? What a curious concept. This planet is swimming in hemoglobin. But let us say that I were marooned on a raft in the middle of the ocean and could not so much as catch a fish. Like any other creature, I would starve. Of course, the real problem would be the sunburn. My skin is quite sensitive.

I try to imagine Draco sitting at his computer. At first I see a tall, dark-haired, handsome man in his thirties. He has cold eyes and a cruel mouth. Like Pierce Brosnan only younger and paler. He is sipping red fluid from a wineglass. I shake my head to clear it. Now I see a pimply twenty-something computer nerd guzzling Yoo-Hoo and scratching himself and pouring a lot of misplaced energy into the net. Some jerk without a life.

Sblood: maybe you should see a doctor, Draco

Draco: How amusing. I did visit a physician recently for a blood workup. I was concerned that I might have become HIV positive. Many of us have contracted AIDS, you see. The sad fact is that the consumption of human nectar, while sublime, is not without risk. This is why I have been raising potbellied pigs

Sblood: did they check your blood glucose? Maybe you've got diabetes.

Draco: Ah, Sweetblood, still promoting your diabetic vampire theory I see. In fact, my blood appeared to be normal in most respects, although the physician seemed a bit concerned about my cholesterol levels

Sblood: too much pork in your diet

Draco: perhaps

2Tooth: How old wre U when U started?

Draco: you mean when I passed? Chaos, upheaval, revelation. I was fifteen.

Sblood: how old are you now?

Draco: That is a very rude question! But I'll provide you with an answer of sorts. When I first felt the Hunger there was no internet, no cell phones, no CDs.

Sblood: were there cars?

Draco: Yes, dear, there were cars.

Here is what I think: I think these cyber-vamps are playing games. If any one of them, including Draco, were to gulp a goblet of pig's blood, I bet he'd puke it right back up again.

I've been all over the Web. Several so-called vampires and vampire groups have sites where they talk about things vampiric. There are psychic vampires and energy vampires and vampire-lifestylers and immortal vampires and a few who just claim to enjoy an occasional taste of blood. Some of them believe in the classic supernatural vampire: creatures that can turn into bats and show no reflection and so forth. Others maintain that vampires are a subspecies of *Homo sapiens*. There are also those who claim that vampires are victims of a retrovirus that requires them to drink blood to survive. And a few see vampirism as a religion or a form of meditation. But most of them, I think, are just posers. They just like to dress up and look cool and act weird.

I mean, maybe a few of the really warped ones drink a little blood now and then, but that doesn't make them real vampires. I could tell them about *real* vampires, but they wouldn't like it any more than Mrs. Graham will when she reads my essay.

I wonder if she's reading it right now.

I really wish I'd left out the impalement stuff.

8

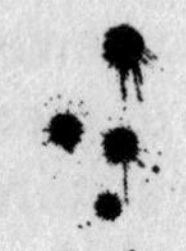

Femmes Fatale

"I have a present for you, Vampire Lady."

Guy is standing in front of me in the hallway. We have just survived another French class. He has a tattoo on his wrist: a red heart pierced by a black sword. I wonder why I didn't notice it before. A small white cardboard box rests in the palm of his hand.

"What is it?" I ask.

"Open it."

I take the box and lift the lid. Inside, resting on a pillow of cotton, is a pale green object about an inch and a quarter long. It is smooth and semi-translucent, as if carved from jade. Its shape that of an imperfect cylinder. One end is bullet-shaped with a tiny black stem in the center; the other end is asymmetrical, like the point of a used green lipstick. A row of tiny metallic gold dots circle one end, looking as if they had been applied by a steady hand with the smallest imaginable paintbrush. I touch it gently with the tip of my finger. It is firm, but not hard like stone. It is neither warm nor cool. I think of plastic, but with a softer, more organic feel.

"What is it?"

"A chrysalis."

For a second I don't get it, but then something from biology class comes back to me.

"You mean, like a cocoon?"

Guy nods. "It's a monarch butterfly. It's alive."

A river of students passes on either side of us, heading for their third-hour classes. I almost lose myself in Guy's blue eyes. I look away.

"You're giving me a bug?"

"Don't you like it?"

"Nobody's ever given me a bug before."

It doesn't take long for Mrs. Graham to call a high-level Saturday morning conference. Buttface, Graham, and my parents are all at the school trying to decide what to do about me, the Evil Bloodsucking Witch Bitch of Seward High. They actually invited me to come, but I declined to participate in my own destruction. I didn't think I could stand to watch my mother wring the skin right off of her hands while my dad sits there with his jaw clamped and his forehead vein pulsing *thump thump thump*.

I'm *ostensibly* (love that word) staying home to work on my French grammar. For example, I have written the following highly grammatical sentences:

Français me fait mal.
Je vais aller au mall.

In case you don't read French, that means: "French makes me sick. I'm going to the mall."

Our city is not a monster metropolis like New York or Los Angeles, but it's big enough to have three high schools and a dozen movie theaters and two colleges and Crosstown Center, an indoor mall with forty-seven shops. The mall isn't exactly Rodeo Drive, but I decide to make a fashion statement anyway.

I put on my makeup. Lots of black around the eyes because I'm in a black mood. I go with the purple lipstick and I add a spot of red to the tips of my black nails.

They want weird, I'll give 'em weird. I look out the window. Leaves are blowing from the trees—it's one of those cloudy fall days that can get cold in a hurry. I opt for a turtleneck (black, of course), my biker jacket with the chain epaulets, and a leather cap that makes me look a little like a goth Marlon Brando before he got old and fat. My boots would really complete the look, but it's a long walk to the mall, so I compromise with a pair of purple high-top sneakers. I consider sunglasses, but since I've done such an awesome job with the eyeliner and mascara I decide to let my eyeballs hang naked.

Before I step outside, I plug into my CD player and I stuff some granola bars and candy into my pockets and I test my blood sugar. The machine sucks in the droplet of blood, thinks about it, then tells me I'm alive, with a slightly elevated blood glucose of 147 mg/dl. Good enough. I'll need the extra glucose for the walk.

Crosstown Center is almost three miles from our house. It's a long walk, but better than sitting around waiting for my parents to come home with a new plan for turning me into somebody I'm not.

I decide to walk the railroad tracks instead of taking Cooley Drive. The tracks are only three blocks from home, and they go right past the mall. Also, I won't run the risk of my parents driving by and seeing me.

I used to play out by the tracks when I was little. Mark Murphy and I would make little houses out of cardboard and mud and set them up on the rails and populate them with tiny stick figures, then we would wait for a train to come by. I guess that was kind of a strange thing to do, but we were just little kids.

One time—I must've been about eight—I was out by the tracks by myself. I remember the smooth metal of the rail, warm from the sun, pressing against my cheek. Maybe I was playing at being an Indian, listening for the sounds of a coming train. I became very sleepy. I curled up on the tracks and drifted.

Sometimes an insulin reaction will sneak up on me like that. The next thing I remember is my mother shrieking, pulling me off the tracks.

"What's the matter with you?" she kept asking.

Well, gee, Mom, I have diabetes and I'm, like, eight years old. Gimme a break!

I understand why she was so upset. If I ever breed (which I definitely do not plan to do) I wouldn't want to find my kid asleep on a railroad track. But I hope I'd be cooler about stuff like that.

So for most of my childhood I was forbidden to go anywhere near the tracks, and mostly I didn't, but I'm not a little kid anymore and it really is the fastest way to get to Crosstown Center.

I walk between the rails, my sneakers hitting every other tie, the wind gusting, pushing me from behind.

Crosstown Center is crowded because of the big sale they always have between the back-to-school sale and the Thanksgiving sale. This year they're calling it Octoberfest. I don't know why they'd name a clothing sale after a German beer-drinking festival, but I guess any excuse will do for a sale. All the stores have tables out front piled high with whatever they most want to get rid of: a lot of ugly sweaters and skirts and shoes and stuff that even Mark Murphy wouldn't be caught dead in. There's some cool stuff, too, but only in midget and monster sizes.

I run into Fiona Cassaday and Marquissa Smith-Valasco sitting by the fountain in the central courtyard. Fiona makes me think of a fairy. She is thin and delicate-looking, with pale, translucent skin and hair the color of blood-tinged water. Her eyes are of a blue so pale that they look almost white, her hands are long and thin.

She looks as if she's been drained by a very thirsty vampire.

"Hey, Luce." Fiona is wearing a leather bomber jacket over a cotton dress with orange and purple stripes like a nightmare candy cane. Her thin legs are crossed, and her feet are encased in clunky-looking red boots. She is smoking a cigarette, which you are not supposed to do in the mall.

Fiona and I have only one thing in common. We are both *très* weird.

"Somebody's going to bust you," I say, pointing at the cigarette.

Fiona smiles with her small teeth, all about the same size. "I *know,*" she says. She looks off to the right.

I follow her glance and see the security guard standing near the information kiosk.

"That's Steve *Monson,* Jimmy Monson's older *brother.*" Fiona has a way of stressing certain words. It's like she's *shooting* them at you. "He's a student at *Harker.*"

Harker College is one of the two colleges in the city.

The guard, Steve *Monson,* is broad-shouldered and erect. His uniform actually looks good on him, which is amazing because the Crosstown Center security guard uniform, with its two-tone pockets, matching epaulets, and short sleeves, is the depth of dork fashion.

"I'm waiting for him to make me put it *out,*" Fiona says. "Don't you think he's *cute*?"

"She's in femme fatale mode," says Marquissa. Marquissa always looks as if she is about to collapse from terminal boredom. Her eyelids are huge and her thick lips never quite close. She has black hair down to her waist, so black it is like a hole in reality. I would kill for hair that black.

"Shut *up*," says Fiona, laughing. Fiona is *always* in femme fatale mode. Fiona has chased guys since the day she was born. She's caught a few, too.

Marquissa turns to me, "Speaking of femme fatale, I saw you talking to Dylan."

"Dylan?" I wrinkle my brow, as if I'm trying to remember. "Oh yeah, he's in my French class."

"He's hot," Marquissa says.

I want to hit her, but I just glare. Marquissa is wearing a black leather trenchcoat. I think she must have stolen it, because those things go for a lot of money. I wish I had one. Marquissa thinks she is this deep dark goth, like she can make flowers wilt by glaring at them. But I knew her before she got her frowny black-leather attitude, back before she changed her name from Mary to

Marquissa. She is so into the goth thing she even wears fishnet on her arms sometimes, which is kind of like a preacher wearing a yellow smiley-face button.

Let me be perfectly clear about one thing: I am not goth. I am Lucy Sweetblood Szabo, and just because I like to dress black and have an unhealthy interest in blood-sucking demons doesn't mean I am some goth fashion junkie who listens to Sisters of Mercy and sleeps with peroxide-soaked sponges to make her face whiter, and has so many buckles, chains, and piercings that she jingles when she walks. Well, maybe I jingle a little. But I'm just me, and anybody who goths me is in big trouble.

"So what are you *doing*?" Fiona asks me.

"Nothing. Just getting the hell out of the house."

"Christ, *tell* me about it. My mom's been on the *warpath* lately."

"My parents are over at the school having a meeting with Graham."

"Graham? *Mrs*. Graham? What did you *do*?"

"I wrote this paper about vampires."

"Vampires? Was it about *Buffy*? Graham *hates* TV."

"No, it was about real vampires. It was kind of bloody."

"Yuck." Fiona frowns at her cigarette, shoots a look at Steve Monson, gets nothing back, drops the butt into the fountain.

"Anyway, it was mostly true stuff," I say.

"What was?" She is glaring at Steve Monson, who is watching a pair of older girls walking into the Gap.

"The vampire stuff. So I don't see what they're so upset about."

"Vampires aren't *real*," Fiona says. "Maybe they think you've gone *nuts*."

Marquissa is watching us talk, her heavily lidded eyes almost closed.

I'm not sure I want to get into the whole vampire thing with Fiona. She's the type who might just spread it all over school and make me out to be even more of a freak than I am.

"They *already* think I'm nuts." Now *I'm* talking like Fiona.

Fiona lights another cigarette.

Marquissa says, "Yes they are."

Fiona blows smoke. "Yes *who* are *what*?"

"Vampires. They're real."

"Yeah, right. I suppose you *know* one?"

"I've met a few," Marquissa says.

Fiona and I look at her.

"These guys I know from Harker are into it. They read every book there is about vampires and watch movies and dress up and do rituals and stuff."

"That doesn't make them vampires."

"They drink blood."

"*Real* blood?" Fiona asks.

"That's what they say," Marquissa says.

"They aren't real vampires," I say. "They're just role-playing."

"How do you know?"

"If they were real you'd never know it. You'd wake up one morning with your throat ripped out."

Fiona looks like she's about to barf. "*You* guys are *disgusting*."

Marquissa smiles sleepily.

9

Low

The clouds are heavy and low as I walk between the tracks. I am staring down. My shoes are purple flashes against the dark brown of railroad ties; the wind is against me, cutting up under my jacket, sucking heat and moisture from my body. I am thinking about what Marquissa said about her so-called vampire friends.

According to Marquissa, these "vampires" get together to talk about vampire books and watch movies. Some of them dress up and even wear fangs. And they drink blood.

"You ever taste it?" I asked.

"Yuck!" she said, scrunching up her face. "It's probably not really blood. I bet they just drink red wine or something, and they tell you it's blood because they don't want you to have any."

"They say it's blood."

I laughed, and Marquissa got all peeved. That was when Steve Monson finally came over and made Fiona put out the cigarette. He was all business and treated us like a bunch of kids. After that we went up to the food court, except I couldn't eat anything because I hadn't brought any insulin with me. I had to sit and drink Diet Coke and watch Fiona and Marquissa wolf down slices of pizza.

Now I'm starving, and still a mile from home. Sometimes it sucks being Undead.

I like my purple shoes. I do not have many nonblack articles of clothing. Maybe I should buy some other purple things. Purple underwear, maybe.

I listen to the *swish swish swish* of my arms swinging, leather on leather, and the *scuff scuff scuff* of rubber soles hitting railroad ties.

My head feels large. The wind fills my ears. My legs are like puppet limbs, loose-hinged and numb as wood. I am having some trouble staying centered on the tracks. I wish they were railings, waist high, something to hang on to.

I am moving very slowly now, as if time is coming to a stop. Something is very wrong. An internal voice says to me, *"Eat something."*

I step off the tracks and walk a few yards to a patch of low grass, moving as if through water; the air is thick and hard to breathe.

"Eat," says the voice.

I dig in my pockets and come out with a granola bar. I would rather have a slice of pizza. I sit down on the grass, staring at the granola bar. When I blink, the wrapper flashes like a strobe light.

"Eat," says the voice.

I tear the end off the wrapper and put one end of the bar in my mouth and bite and chew. It is dry, like sawdust. I chew and swallow. A box of cranberry juice would be nice. Bite, chew, swallow. Am I sitting on the railroad tracks? No, I can see the tracks, far away, as if through the wrong end of a telescope. The edges of my vision are dark as charcoal. My mind stops. I stare thoughtlessly at a stalk of dry goldenrod quivering in the wind. Yellow leaves tumble by, but my eyes are frozen. Time passes. After a few eons my mind begins to work again. I have the empty granola bar wrapper in my hand. I must have eaten the whole thing. That is good. Words form on the movie screen in my head, explanatory subtitles appear:

LUCY HAVING ANOTHER INSULIN REACTION.
LUCY DIGESTING GRANOLA BAR.
CARBOHYDRATES ARE CONVERTED BY LIVER TO GLUCOSE.
BLOOD SUGAR RISES.

I cross my arms; I hug myself. My guts feel disconnected. That was a bad one. I could have passed out. I almost did. I feel stupid. I am shivering. I should have eaten the granola bar before leaving the mall, but I was so busy feeling sorry for myself because I couldn't have any pizza that I forgot about the calories I'd need for the walk home.

Being a proto-vampire means constantly balancing food and insulin and exercise. Too many cookies and the blood sugar soars, a little too much insulin and it drops, producing an insulin reaction. Exercise also affects blood sugar. If I exercise without eating, I risk having a reaction.

Every insulin reaction is different. Usually they are no big deal. I feel kind of weird, I drink a glass of juice, and everything goes back to normal. But some of them are almost like a religious experience, complete with hallucinations, bizarre thoughts, and disturbing physical sensations.

I don't know how long I've been sitting here, but the sky is lower and darker now and the wind has picked up. My head is pounding. Insulin reactions often give me a headache. I'm trembling from the cold. I stand up. I'm still a little dizzy, but I start walking, one step at a time.

There is a special feeling that comes when you are cold and hungry and it is dark, and you see the shape of your house and lights in the windows, and then you are home. You open the door and the warm, moist smell of cooking hits you. You peel off your jacket and the heat floods in through your pores and you are safe.

When I walk into the house I'm not thinking about being late for dinner or about Mrs. Graham or any of my other troubles. I just feel good to be safe and warm and home.

That lasts for about three seconds.

"Sweetie? Is that you, Honey?"

"It's me."

She appears in the kitchen doorway, twisting a dish towel in her hands.

"Your father is out looking for you. We were worried."

If she's so worried, why doesn't she give me a hug? Instead, we face off: the evil sugar-bitch daughter and the whiny hand-wringing mother.

"Well, I'm home," I say.

"Your father is very upset."

Now I'm not so hungry anymore. I head for the stairs.

"Sweetie?"

I ignore the whine and take the steps two at a time. When I close the door to my room I feel safe. I flop back on my bed and stare up at Rubber Bat and, above him, the Seven Sisters. They are dark maroon now, but I remember when they were scarlet and fresh. That was months ago. I'd been sitting on my bed testing my blood sugar, but when I lanced my finger I must've gone too deep because a jet of blood shot into the air like Old Faithful, leaving seven bright, wet, red droplets suspended from the textured ceiling. I have named them the seven sisters of the Pleiades: Halcyone, Taygete, Asterope, Celæno, Electra, Maia, and Merope. I was really into Greek mythology for about five minutes once.

I wonder where my father is. He knows nothing about me, so he is probably driving aimlessly, all serious and fatherly. My head is still pounding. Should I risk a trip to the bathroom to get an aspirin? I decide against it. They'll probably leave me alone for a while if I stay in my room. If I pretend to be doing homework. I sit up and go to my desk and reach to turn on my computer but my hand swipes air. For a moment I am confused—am I having another insulin reaction?

Slowly, I sit down. This is no insulin reaction. This is far, far worse.

I stare at the empty space where my computer used to be.

10

BLAH BLAH BLAH

Shouting doesn't work. Neither does sulking or refusing to talk. But I try it for a day anyway. The next night at supper, after 24 hours of Lucy Locklip, I offer them a deal.

"Deal?" My father's eyebrows jump so high I'm looking for his eyelids to rip, and his mouth is squirming—I don't know if it's a snarl or a suppressed laugh. "What sort of deal, Sport?"

"You give me my computer back and I'll listen to what you have to say."

He laughs. I stare back at him stone-faced.

My mother says, "Sweetie—"

"Please don't call me that."

"Honey—"

"Or Honey or Sugar. Or *Sport*." I shoot a look at my father. "My name is Lucy."

"Young lady"—he is less amused now—"I don't think you understand just how much trouble you're in."

"What? Because I wrote a highly historically accurate essay? Because I'm having one bad semester at school? Because I was a few minutes late for dinner one night?"

He's shaking his head. "Settle down, Lucy. Just . . . settle."

I realize that I'm standing up, waving my fork and screaming. I'd promised myself I wouldn't do that. I take a breath and sit down and fold my hands in my lap.

"Sorry."

"Listen to what we have to say, then we'll talk about giving you back your computer."

"It's mine. You should just give it to me."

He shakes his head, wearing his stone face. I see that I'm not going to change it easily.

"Okay," I say, "talk."

My father did most of the talking.

"The first thing we want you to know is that we love you very much, and we want what is best for you."

Inside my head I reply, *BLAH BLAH*

BLAH—then why did you breed a kid with diabetes?

"And we're worried about you."

I am keeping my face very still.

"Mrs. Graham is worried too."

BLAH BLAH BLAH.

"You know, when someone you love seems to change suddenly, it's a little scary. Last year you seemed to be doing so well at school, and now . . . well, you seem so unhappy."

***BLAH BLAH BLAH**. How happy would you be if you were a teenage diabetic vampire freak?*

"And that *essay* you wrote—," my mother breaks in.

My father shuts her up with a glance. He says, "It's not the essay, Lucy. Not just that. I mean, we know that Mrs. Graham is kind of old-fashioned. And I know you just wrote that to shock her—"

"I wrote it because it's true," I said.

"Well . . . you don't really think you're a *vampire*," he says.

I stare back at him. I want to say, *Yes, I really do think I'm a bloodsucking demon from hell.* But I know if I say *that* I'll *never* get my computer back.

I say, "Not really."

He looks relieved. "Good." He leans

forward and puts on his friendly concerned-dad face. "The reason we took your computer, Lucy, is because of some of the Web sites you've been visiting. I checked them out."

"Excuse me? You went snooping in my computer?"

"I looked at your Internet history file. I visited some of those sites, Lucy. The vampire sites? You know, there are some very sick, dangerous people out there."

"It's just role-playing."

"Most of it is, I agree, but not all. I believe that some of those people are very serious."

"I don't *think* so."

"Well, I do. A girl . . . a young *woman* like you . . . you have to be careful. There are a lot of predators out there."

"So you *do* believe in vampires?"

He sits back and crosses his arms. Not a good sign.

"Okay, okay! What do you want me to do?" I ask.

They look at each other—another bad sign. The arms uncross and he is leaning in on me again.

"Lucy, we want you to be safe and happy."

I don't know what he's going to say next. But I know I'm not gonna like it.

❧

My parents want me to see a counselor. A shrink. They don't want me to be a vampire, so they are sending me to a headshrinker. I imagine a leering, wrinkled old man asking questions about my sex life. He won't find much there.

The guy they want me to see is a psychologist recommended by Buttface.

"Forget it," I say.

"I don't think you understand," my father says after a few seconds. "You really don't have a choice here." His face is hard as stone. I can hardly believe this is the same man I used to trade winks with. If he winked now I think his eyelid would crack.

"You mean if I don't see your shrink you'll have me committed or something?"

They just stare at me. Uh-oh. I think furiously.

"I'll talk to Fish," I say.

"Fish?"

"Dr. Fisher."

My mother jumps in. "But . . . Honey . . . Dr. Fisher is an *endocrinologist*."

"He's a *doctor*. Look, I've got an appointment this week for my six-month checkup. I'll talk to him, and if he thinks I need a shrink, then I'll go."

"I really don't think this is Dr. Fisher's

area of expertise," my father says.

"Maybe my problem is diabetes related." I can see they aren't buying that. "Besides, if I have to see a shrink, I'd rather see somebody recommended by Fish than by Buttface."

"Lucy!" my mother says. At least she didn't call me HoneySweetieSugar again.

They don't like it, but after a bit of stubborn squalling, they agree. In the meantime, I'm off-line and grounded. They also decide to deprive me of telephone privileges, just to be extra cruel.

It feels a lot like being really, truly dead.

Since all of my other evening options suck worse, I decide to do my laundry. I've been washing my own clothes for the past six months, ever since I complained about the way my mother folded my jeans. But that was another crisis, another time.

I'm going through my pockets when I come across something hard and square. The box that Guy gave to me. With my life turning into a disaster movie, I'd forgotten all about it. I open it carefully, not sure whether I'll find a chrysalis, a butterfly, or something else altogether. To my relief, the green chrysalis is resting comfortably on its spun-cotton pillow. I hold it in my hand and look closely at the smooth, green, waxy surface. The gold dots are a little brighter than I remember them. Can it really be alive?

I am reminded of something. When Mark Murphy and I were little kids we would catch fireflies and, at the moment of illumination, pinch off their rear ends and stick the glowing guts on the backs of our fingers. We called it night jewelry. One time we got pretend-married and gave each other firefly wedding rings. Of course, the night jewelry—and our marriage—only lasted a few minutes. After that all we had was firefly guts.

There is a small black stem on one end of the chrysalis. I attach a piece of tape to the stem and hang it from the shelf above my computerless computer desk and think about Guy. Dylan. I don't know which name I like better. I close my honey-colored eyes and think about his blues and wonder if maybe he is the one who will complete me. I have always thought that I am only part of a person, and that there is someone out there who will fit to me the way a key fits a lock. But what kind of guy would give me a bug for a present? Is this a teenage version of getting pretend-married with firefly guts?

I separate my darks from my lights—the dark pile is way bigger—and I carry them downstairs to the laundry room.

11

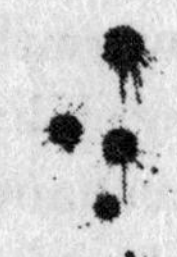

French Cuisine

Monday, in mourning for my missing computer, I dress in black. Of course, I always dress in black, but this morning I dress even blacker than usual. I put on my black wool turtleneck and let the long sleeves hang over my hands all the way to my freshly painted all-black nails. I wear black jeans that I over-dyed to make them even blacker, and my black suede boots, and my black raincoat (even though it isn't raining) and my eyeshadow and my blackest, inkiest, foulest attitude. My goal is to get through the entire day without saying a word to anyone.

I head out the door and up Birch Street toward the high school. Leaves swirl around on the sidewalk, caught in invisible whirlpools. Wind sneaks in beneath my raincoat. The sun squints between clouds, glows weakly for a few seconds, then slips back into hiding before a single BTU of warmth can reach my bones. I am feeling very chilly and dark when my ex-pretend-husband Mark Murphy comes jogging up, all cheerful and sunny.

"Hey, Skeeter!"

I would ignore him, but Mark and I go too far back. So much for my day of silence.

"Morning, Monkey," I say.

"You're looking extra spooky today."

"Thank you. I'm feeling spooky."

"Getting ready for Halloween?"

"Not exactly." I look at his Seward High letter jacket, orange with blue leather sleeves. "Are you?"

He laughs.

I say, "I'm in mourning. My parents took away my computer."

"How come?"

"They think I'm getting too weird."

Mark doesn't say anything.

"I am, you know."

"You am what?"

"Weird."

Mark's jacket looks huge on his lanky frame. He got his letter in track. Mark is a sprinter, and he runs hurdles. Even though

I think sports are stupid, I once watched one of his track meets. Mark took second place in the 100-meter event. It was strange seeing the goofy, jolly Mark Murphy being so serious and focused and *fast*. In those eleven seconds I saw something inside him. Something tough and determined and a little bit scared.

I'm that way too. Except I'm not always so tough.

"What did you do?" he asks.

"I'm flunking a couple classes."

"You?" He stops and stares at me like I've turned inside out. I keep walking.

"They're boring."

"Wow." He takes three giant strides to catch up. "Why did they take your computer?"

"I wrote this paper—about vampires and stuff? And Mrs. Graham freaked, and then my dad got into my computer and checked out some of the vampire Web sites I'd been at, and they *all* freaked."

"Vampires?"

"Yeah. You know. Bloodsucking demons?"

"I know what vampires are."

I wonder how Mark might react if I tell him I am one. I decide not to.

Neither of us say anything for a while. We are three blocks from school when he finally opens his mouth again.

"You seem kind of unhappy lately," he says.

Now I stop and look at him. "Why should I be happy?"

"I don't know. I just . . ." He is floundering. Like most boys, he has difficulty expressing himself in plain English.

"Do I have something to be happy about?" Putting the pressure on, making him squirm. He looks so uncomfortable.

"I mean . . . is there anything I can do?" He looks pained. "You want to borrow my class notes or anything?"

I laugh at him. It's mean, but I laugh anyway. I've seen Mark's notes. They're nothing short of a disaster. Mark is not exactly honor roll material.

"At least I'm not flunking," he says. I can see I've stung him.

"Notes aren't my problem," I say.

"Oh. So what are you gonna do?"

"I haven't figured that out yet," I say. We are passing beneath a black walnut tree; the sidewalk is littered with fallen nuts in their green and black husks. They look like organic golfballs. I kick one. As it skitters down the walk, the husk disintegrates and the walnut tumbles free, small, black, and hard as a rock. "Maybe I'm nuts," I say.

I slog through the gray day like Godzilla through Tokyo, breathing fire at everybody. Things go from bad to awful on the way to chemistry, when I see Dylan in the hall talking to Marquissa Smith-Valasco. I stop dead. A couple of freshman girls crash into me from behind, spilling my books. Dylan looks up, then comes over to help me pick them up. I don't even say thank you. Marquissa watches, smirking.

In chemistry class I get hungry and eat a granola bar right there at my desk. BoreAss sees me munching and gets upset, making some sarcastic remark. I don't know if he wants me to spit it out, or what.

"I'm having a hypoglycemic episode," I say through a mouthful of granola.

He glares at me, trying to figure out whether I'm lying, which I am.

"Maybe you should go see the nurse," he says.

That sounds good to me. I get up—all eyes on me, waiting for me to collapse or turn to smoke or something—and I walk out. But instead of going to the nurse's office I go to the auditorium.

The school auditorium is big enough to seat every kid at Seward. That's about eleven hundred students. But right now it is empty and semidark, the only light coming from a few dimly lit wall sconces. I walk to the front and climb up onto the stage and sit at the edge and stare out over the seats. It is quiet except for the sound of air molecules on my eardrums, the roar of blood rushing through my veins, and a distant thumping sound. Is it my heart? No, the sound is too irregular. I listen carefully and finally decide I'm hearing the sound of a basketball being dribbled. The gymnasium is right next door.

Every seat in the auditorium has held hundreds of human bodies. I wonder if anything stays. When we sit in a place for a while, does some little tiny fragment of soul remain behind? I imagine each seat filled with multiple ghosts, all of them watching me, waiting for me to do something. If I squint my eyes I can almost see them, like swirls of ice-cold smoke. A prickle runs up my spine and I turn quickly, but the creature behind me is invisible. I close my eyes and imagine Guy appearing from stage left, sitting down next to me, putting his arm around me. Warm. I feel his tattoo touching my shoulder and his breath in my hair and I hear the beating of his heart.

The bell rings, followed by the dull roar of a thousand students moving from the classrooms to the hallways. I hop off the stage and emerge from the peaceful dark and merge with the babbling stream.

Mme. D'Ormay has us break into groups. We are supposed to discuss, in French, our dinner plans. I end up in a group with Gustave, Jean-Claude, René, and Guy. We sit in a small circle, knee to knee. I look down at their motley collection of athletic shoes and my black boots and I feel Guy's blue eyes on me.

Jean-Claude starts things off by saying, *"Je voudrais homard et cravates pour dîner."*

"You're having lobster and neckties for dinner?" I ask.

He blushes. "No. I mean, what's the word for shrimp?"

"Crevettes," I say.

And so it goes. Gustave and René both decide to have *steak au poivre* for dinner. Guy wants *poisson et frites*—his way of saying fish and chips—and I decide to go for the *boudin noir,* or blood sausage. *Ooh-la-la!*

Guy's knee keeps bumping mine. The place where they touch feels hot, like sunburn. I can see his tattoo peeking out from his shirtsleeve, the hilt of the sword and the red tip of the heart. René and Jean-Claude are discussing appetizers. They are getting goofy. René is insisting on *escargot,* while Jean-Claude wants *les oeufs du lapin étouffée* (stuffed rabbit eggs). Guy leans over and whispers to me, "You want to head over to Harker Village after school? Grab a latte and something to eat? Snails or something?"

"Can't," I say.

We return to our weird meal plans.

After class, in the hall, Guy stops me. His blue eyes pin me to the wall. "You sure? I'll buy you a cappuccino at the Bean."

"I told you. I can't. Why don't you ask Marquissa?"

"Marquissa?" He looks puzzled. "Why would I do that?"

I look away, embarrassed now. "Anyway, I'm grounded. My parents have got me under house arrest."

He says, "How can they do that? You're almost an adult."

"I'm sixteen."

"A couple hundred years ago you'd already be married and have kids."

"A couple hundred years ago I'd be dead." *Sweetened to death.*

"Really?"

"Yeah." *Or maybe with a stake through my heart.*

"I thought vampires lived forever."

"I'm of the mortal variety."

Guy laughs. The halls are emptying as kids filter into classrooms.

"I gotta go," I say.

12

Poisson

Fish—Harlan Fisher, M.D.—is a very handsome man, but old. His temples are gray, and the crow's-feet at the corners of his eyes have more toes than a centipede. I'm sure he's older than my parents, and they're almost fifty. This afternoon, Fish is wearing jeans and a yellow shirt, with the sleeves rolled up to show off his hairy arms. You would never guess that he's a doctor except for the stethoscope. He grins at me as he enters the examination room.

"What's up, Lucinda Szabo?"

"That's *Ms.* Lucinda Szabo, to you."

"Oh-ho! In a mood today, are we? How have your blood sugars been?"

I tell him, lying only a little bit, which he

expects. He goes through the usual list of questions, making notes on my chart. He chides me for my last glycosylated hemoglobin—that's the test for long-term blood sugar level—and congratulates me for having a pulse. He keeps up a steady stream of chatter as he checks my feet for signs of neuropathy and looks in my eyes for signs of retinopathy. If I didn't know better I would say he is nervous.

I'm waiting for an opportunity to say something about my problem with my parents, but it's not an easy thing to get into. Maybe I'll say nothing, then tell my parents that Fish said I don't need a shrink. Would they buy it? I don't think so.

"Hello? Earth to Ms. Szabo?" Fish is staring at me.

"What?"

"I asked you how school was going." He backs off and sits down at his swivel chair.

"Oh. Okay, I guess."

"I heard different. From your mother. She called this morning."

"Oh. Well, it's not going *that* okay. Basically, I'm flunking out."

"I thought you were Ms. 'Straight A' Szabo."

"An older version of me," I say, quoting Alanis Morrisette.

"I see." He waits.

"Actually, it was this paper I wrote that got me in trouble."

"Oh?"

"You remember last time I was here I told you my vampire theory?"

Fish has very nice, large, even teeth, but they are kind of yellow. "You mean about vampire legends being based on untreated diabetics?"

"Yeah."

He chuckles. "You know, I ran that theory by a few of my colleagues. They got a kick out of it."

"That's because it's probably true."

"It could very well be," Fish says. "Not that anyone will ever be able to prove it."

"I could go off my insulin and see what happens."

"I wouldn't recommend that!"

"Just for a few weeks. You know. See if my teeth grow."

Fish is peering at me with his eyebrows all scrunched together. He's not sure I'm kidding.

I say, "Who knows? Maybe the cure for diabetes is to drink the blood of normal people. An old Transylvanian cure?"

Fish's eyebrows do another contortion, then he forces out a laugh: HA HA HA.

"Do you want a prescription for that?" he asks, trying to join me in the joke. I can see that he is uncomfortable. That makes me mad, so I just stare back at him without smiling. He looks down at my chart for a few seconds, then changes the subject.

"What was the paper you wrote that got you in so much trouble?"

"I just wrote out my theory. And added some background information. You know—stuff about Vlad the Impaler and Elizabeth Bathory. Kind of nasty stuff. But mostly I just described how this diabetic girl turns into a vampire and eats her neighbors' stew and then gets burned to death by some angry villagers."

Fish nods. "Sounds gruesome. I take it your teacher didn't like your theory?"

"Well, she called my parents . . . and you know how *they* are. They already think I'm some sort of bad seed, what with my diabetes and being a teenager and all."

"You really think that?"

"I think they don't know what to make of me."

"Okay, you wrote a paper that didn't go over so well. How come you're having so much trouble in your other classes?"

"Ennui," I say.

"On wee?"

"Oui."

Fish laughs. It's not that funny, but I laugh too. It's been a while.

I say, "Look, school's just really tedious right now. I got straight As for, like, three years in a row. I don't see why everybody freaks out if I slack off for one semester. What's the big deal? School is boring."

"You know, it's not such an awful thing to be bored."

"Easy for you to say. You're old."

"I wasn't always. Look at it this way. School is boring no matter how you cut it, right?"

"Mostly."

"Would it be any more boring if you did the work?"

"It might not be more boring, but it would be more work."

Fish says nothing, but his look accuses me. I feel pressure building up behind my eyeballs.

"I just don't want to study all the time. I'm sick of it. It's too hard, and it's not fair."

"Why is it not fair?" He seems genuinely puzzled.

"My parents took away my computer. Plus, I have to deal with insulin reactions, and my blood sugars going crazy every time I get my period, and all the rest of it. My parents don't get it at all. My mom's on this huge guilt trip because I got diabetes and my dad, all he can think about when he looks at me is how come I'm not a boy. You know how come I don't have any brothers or sisters? I'll tell you—my mom actually told me this—she said the reason they quit having kids was because they didn't want to risk bringing another diabetic child into the world. Can you imagine her saying that to me? That's my mom."

My eyes are stinging. Hot wet streaks run down my face. I'm sure my cheeks are black with makeup.

Fish is staring at me, his face a cautious blank. He probably wishes he was on the golf course or the moon or anyplace else in the universe, but he is stuck in this examination room with a crazy crying teenage girl vampire. I allow myself a loud snuffle, then I shut off the faucet.

"I just want them to leave me alone," I say.

"Like Greta Garbo," says Fish.

"Who?"

"Greta Garbo, the famous movie star. When she gave up acting back in the 1940s, she told a reporter, 'I want to be left alone.'"

"Did she get what she wanted?"

"I don't know."

⁂

Fish says he will talk to my parents. I don't know if that's good or bad. I trust Fish, but not 100 percent. Maybe he is going to tell them to lock me up.

He sends me to the lab for tests. The lab vampire—she calls herself a phlebotomist—sucks out a few tubes of blood, covers the single fang mark with a bandage, and sends me away. It's a few minutes after one when I leave the clinic, time to get back to school for English, but I really don't want to see Mrs. Graham. Instead, I walk the ten blocks to Harker Village, an area near the college with lots of shops and restaurants. As usual, I stop at Antoinette's Body Art to look at the tattoo designs in the window. Antoinette is sitting outside her door, smoking a cigar. She sees me coming and gives me a little wave.

"Hey, girl," she says. Antoinette is about fifty years old, I think, with short gray hair, huge breasts, huge belly, huge everything. She's been a tattoo artist for twenty years, and she knows everything about everybody. Today she is wearing her favorite outfit: jeans and a black leather vest with dozens of pockets. She has about fifty tattoos on her thick arms and shoulders. Half of them are small black crosses, all the same size. "Still shopping?" she asks.

I look at the hundreds of tattoo designs displayed in the front window—everything from bloody swords to pink roses to shattered skulls to Bugs Bunny. At one time or another I've considered each and every one of them. I've imagined a fiery dragon wrapped around my left arm, a butterfly on my shoulder.

"Yeah. I've heard they don't wash off."

"Not without one hell of a lot of scrubbing," she says with a grin. Antoinette and I have had this conversation dozens of times. She finds me amusing.

"Maybe I'll get an armlet. A chain design wrapped around my arm. You know—to symbolize my enslavement."

"When did you become a slave?"

"When I was born?"

"Really! You are one pissed-off chick."

"I'm not pissed-off. Angry."

"Oh. Well, that's different then. What are you angry about?"

"Everything."

Antoinette puffs on her cigar and gives me a squinty-eyed look through the smoke.

"I used to be like that," she says. She holds out her left arm and points at a tattoo, a flaming skull. "That's how I feel when I'm angry. You want one like that?"

"Uh, not today, thanks."

"Yeah? Well, you decide what you want,

then come back and see me." She flicks her cigar into the gutter. "In the meantime, lighten up, kid. Don't get stuck on yourself. Life is change. Have some fun."

The Sacred Bean is just down the block from Antoinette's. I decide to stop in for a coffee. Who knows? Maybe Guy will stop by. I order a triple cappuccino and sit at the back corner table and brood—something I do well. (I am a world-class brooder; I am the Tiger Woods of brooding.) I don't expect the caffeine to stop the brooding, but it might make me brood faster. I stare across the room, out the glass front door at the fire-red leaves of a maple tree, and try to figure out what is going on with me.

I used to like school.

My parents didn't used to bother me so much.

I used to know how to have fun.

Life didn't used to suck.

Just after school started, I made these complaints to Buttface the counselor. She told me it was normal to feel that way. She said it's part of growing up. Big help there. Now, a few weeks later, I still feel the same way, only now she wants me to see a shrink.

I might be nuts, but at least I'm consistent.

The clock on the wall says 3:05. School's out. I'm grounded. I'm supposed to be on my way home.

A couple of kids I recognize come in and order coffees and take them over by the windows. Maple leaves float down past the glass, flakes of frozen fire. I watch the front door, my cappuccino reduced to a glob of barely warm sludge in the bottom of my cup. I wonder if Guy will show up. Of course, he has no idea that I'm here. I told him I was grounded, that I couldn't meet him. But now here I am, at the Bean, waiting for him.

13

Night Creature

I don't get home until almost five, but my mother is only moderately perturbed. I go straight to my room. My computer has not magically reappeared, but the chrysalis has changed color. It is slightly bluer, like the color of spruce needles. I see faint shadows beneath its surface, dark, parallel lines. I watch it, trying to imagine the consciousness inside. I think how it would feel to bind myself into a cocoon, to metamorphose, to become a Lucy . . . *plus.* I might grow wings, or the hard, chitinous shell of a beetle, or the powerful stinger of a wasp. I once read a story about a man who woke up and found he had turned into a giant cockroach. I would prefer to change into something not quite so creepy-crawly.

I should check my blood sugar, I think. Sometimes when I have weird thoughts—like turning into a bug—it means my glucose is out of whack. Maybe that triple cappuccino kicked it up into the 400s. Or the long walk home brought it down into the thirties. Where it is now, nobody knows. I write down a number on a scrap of paper: 112. I want my blood sugar to be 112. A nice, normal, nondiabetic number. A number that I won't have to bring down with an insulin shot or raise by stuffing food in my face.

I take out my blood glucose meter and stare at its chipped, worn plastic surfaces. This meter has been like a detached part of my body for years. It has analyzed gallons of my sweet, rich blood. Every time I feed it a warm red droplet, it judges me mercilessly. I've been good or I've been bad. Perfect or flawed. Virtuous or wicked. Saintly or sinful. Black or white. The meter will only deliver hard, cold numbers. It won't say, *"You're a little bit high this afternoon, Luce, but not too bad considering what you've been through. I understand completely. Besides, I could be wrong."*

Meters are not like that. I decide not to test. I don't need another hole in my fingertip. Besides, maybe my blood sugar *is* 112. Why waste a test?

I am furious at Guy. I know it's stupid—I told him I couldn't meet him—but I'm mad at him anyway for not showing up at the Bean. Things are happening in my head, angry little explosions leaving vapor trails of thought. Three times I reach to turn on my computer, but it's never there. I put a Concrete Blonde disc in my Discman and my headphones in my ears and lie back on my bed and crank the volume high enough to obliterate thought. I am swallowed by Johnette Napolitano's husky, shredded voice.

I am awakened by headphones being yanked from my head and the harsh sound of my father's voice shouting in my ear. My ears ringing from the headphones, I try to decode his shouted words.

"ARE YOU ALL RIGHT?" He pulls me upright by my arm.

"What are you DOING?" I yell. "Let GO of me!" I jerk my arm from his grasp and flop back onto the bed. My mother is behind him, doing her hand-wringing thing.

"Sweetie . . . ," she says.

"Are you sure you're all right?" my father growls.

"I'm FINE. I just fell asleep. What do you WANT?"

"You didn't answer when I called you for dinner," my mother says.

"Or when we knocked," my father adds.

"We were afraid you . . . we thought maybe you weren't feeling well, Honey."

"Going to ruin your ears with that!" My father thrusts his index finger at my Discman, the headphones still blasting.

I turn off the CD player. We glare at each other like dogs trying to decide if they want to fight. I open my mouth to snarl something but catch myself just in time. If I lose it with them now, I might end up in some institution.

"So . . . what's for dinner?" I ask.

Over dinner, I find out that Fish is just as bad as the rest of them. My parents tell me that he wants me to see a psychologist. Some guy named Carlson, a specialist in adolescent behavior. Dr. Carlson is going to "evaluate" me. *Evaluate*. That's where they tell you if you have any *value*—or if you're a worthless human being. My father tells me this as if he is giving me wonderful news. He has already made an appointment for me.

"We'll get this thing figured out in no time, Sport. Dr. Fisher says Dr. Carlson is one of the best."

My mother's oven-roasted sliced potatoes,

normally one of my favorites, taste like disks of greasy brown corrugated cardboard. I chew and swallow. Chew and swallow. When I can't swallow any more, I excuse myself and return to my room.

I stare up at Rubber Bat and the Seven Sisters and I listen to the murmur of my parents talking over the remains of dinner. My ears are very, very sharp. Like my grandmother used to say, I can hear a mouse walking on velvet. I can't pick out the individual words, but I know they are talking about me. After a while the conversation lags. I hear the soft clatter of dishes going into the sink, the hiss of running water, the rattle and clack of the dishwasher being loaded. Washing dishes used to be my job, but a few weeks back I just quit doing it. It was really weird. I expected some sort of scene, but my mother never said a word; she just took over, as if all the times I'd done them meant nothing, as if I hadn't really mattered.

I imagine how she looks now with her hands plunged in the soapy water. Have I ever mentioned that my mother used to be beautiful? She keeps a photo on her vanity. In the photo she is twenty-four years old. She has long blond hair and she looks happy, as if life could not possibly be better. That was before she had me. She looks different now: brow semiscrunched, half smile, forced cheeriness, and that haunted, scared look in her eyes. I know what she's scared of. She's scared of her daughter, the wicked protovampire Lucinda. Wherever I go, whatever I am doing, I see her face accusing me. I see her hands washing my dishes. I want to say, *This wasn't my idea. I didn't ask to be born.*

Finally there is a brief silence, then the sharper sound of electronic chatter from the den. My parents, intellectual giants, watch about four hours of TV every night. They will stare at it until it's time to go to bed. I wait until they are completely hypnotized, then sneak downstairs and get my father's cell phone out of his coat pocket. I creep back up to my room and call information. There are only three Redfields listed. I get the right one on the second try.

"Hello?"

I recognize Guy's voice right away.

"Where were you?" I say.

"Who is this?"

"This is the grounded vampire."

"Lucy?"

"Where were you? I went to the Bean, but you weren't there."

"I thought you were grounded."

"So?" I'm not going to make this easy for

him. If he really likes me, he'll have to learn to deal.

"Sorry—I didn't think you'd be there."

"Well, I was."

"Oh."

"You know what I'm doing right now?"

"Talking on the phone?"

"I'm looking at that bug you gave me."

"Yeah? Is it doing anything?"

"It's just sort of hanging out. Where'd you get it?"

"I have my sources. Hey, you want to go over to the Bean? They're open till two. They have live music at night."

"Can't," I say. "I'm grounded."

Guy doesn't say anything for a couple of seconds, then, in a tentative voice, he asks, "Does that mean that I should go to the Bean anyway, just in case you decide to go—even though you can't go because you're grounded? Or do you mean you really can't go? Which is it?"

"Yes," I say. I hang up.

I can be a real bitch sometimes.

Twenty minutes later I feel bad. I call Guy to tell him I was just kidding, but a woman answers—his mother, I suppose—and tells me he went out. I hang up before she asks who I am. I flop back on my bed and imagine him sitting at the same table I was at, sipping cappuccino and watching the door. Serve him right. At the same time, I know that I'm being completely unfair. I lay there letting the thoughts swirl around in my head. After a while I go downstairs and return the phone to my dad's coat pocket and wander into the den. The parents are zombied-out, watching a rerun of *Little House on the Prairie,* my mother's favorite show.

"Hey," I say.

Heads turn.

"You think you could turn it down a little? I'm going to sleep."

Wordlessly, my father lifts the remote and lowers the volume.

"Thanks," I say.

I go back to my room. Now that I've announced that I'm going to bed, they won't look in on me.

I put on my black denim shirt with the silver buttons. I touch up my eyeliner and layer on a fresh coat of lipstick and run a brush through my hair and add a few rings to my fingers and grab my black cotton trench coat and climb out the window and down the antenna post to the ground like the predatory creature of the night that I am. I head up the dark side of the street, the long tails of the trench coat flapping behind me.

14

Espresso Yourself

The frowning barista has a bone in her nose. It looks like the short end of a wishbone from a Thanksgiving turkey, and it is stuck right through her left nostril like somebody stabbed her with it. The pointy end is hanging over her upper lip. I think it must be hard for her to talk. No wonder she is unhappy. I order a triple latte. While she hisses and foams, I look around.

The Bean is different at night. Different crowd; not so Joe College. I see a lot of leather but very few books. I am looking for Guy, but there are too many black-leather-jacketed, black-haired guys. Cigarette smoke hangs in a layer about four feet off the floor. The room is lit by a dozen tiny halogen track lights scattered across the dark ceiling: an upside-down field of miniature searchlights cutting through nicotine fog. It's hard to see across the room.

The barista pushes my latte at me with a boney frown. I pay her. She gives me change. I say, "Thank you." The barista says nothing. I wonder why she is so unhappy, and why she has chosen to stick an ugly old turkey bone in her nose. Maybe it is an act. Maybe she doesn't know how to act, so she sticks a bone in her nostril and acts pissed-off. I've been there. Only without the bone.

I add four packets of fake sugar to my latte, then go looking for a table where I can sit and act blasé. I find one near the small stage, where two tall, pale, stringy-haired, blue-lipsticked women are setting up. They look like sisters. One of them has a big stand-up bass, the other an oboe. I sit and sip. The blue lips are talking, but I can't understand what they are saying. After a few moments of confusion, I realize that they are speaking another language, and suddenly I feel ultrahip and worldly sitting with my triple latte late at night surrounded by black leather and cigarette smoke and women speaking a strange tongue. So what if Guy doesn't show? I am my own cool self.

I can sit here and be a part of this scene even though I'm only in high school and I don't know anybody and I can't imagine what these two blue-lipped women are planning to do with a bass and an oboe.

I am halfway through my latte when I find out. Without ceremony, the oboist sister begins to play. The sound is deep and pure and rich, tingling the fine hairs on my arms, a falling series of notes like the calling of an owl. She repeats the series again and again, each time with some tiny variation: a little slower, a little quieter, a little harsher. A contest of owls? I close my eyes and I am flying through the forest at night, hooting. Then the bass notes hit: I feel the thrumming in my lips and my breasts. Startled, I look at the bass player. She is staring at me, a faint curve on her blue lips, long fingers slapping fat strings. I close my eyes and let the raw sound carry me away. I am flying again, sliding through the woods on liquid air, leaves stroking my body like fronds of seaweed. Maybe I am not an owl. Maybe I am some other night creature. I twist and turn in midair; the full moon flashes through the foliage. If I knew where I was I could fly across town to the Sacred Bean and see myself through the window, sitting here with my eyes closed, absorbing the sounds of oboe and bass.

My imagination is quite real, quite intense. It has gotten me through many an algebra class.

The bass vibrations cease. The hooting of the oboe slows, quiets, then stops altogether. My ears are again filled with the chatter of multiple conversations. I open my eyes to find Guy sitting across from me, his blue eyes fixed upon my honey browns.

"I'm surprised you came," I say.

Guy nods. On the tiny stage behind him the blue-lipped women are sharing a cigarette, taking a break. Guy is holding a tiny espresso cup.

"I can't stay very long," I say.

Guy sips his espresso. His tattoo peeks at me from beneath the cuff of his leather jacket. I sip my latte—I *try* to sip my latte—but my mug is empty and all I get is a glob of foam on my lip.

"You want another one?" Guy asks.

"No, thank you."

One corner of his mouth turns up. "You are very polite," he says. He is sitting directly beneath one of the track lights. His thick black hair glistens.

"But I'll take an espresso," I say. I don't

want him to think I'm *too* polite. Also, I need to get rid of him for a couple minutes so I can think.

He melts into the sea of black leather, and I frantically try to imagine how the rest of the evening will go.

My brain freezes; I fail.

He is back with my espresso. I take the tiny cup in my hands and hold it up to my nose and inhale. The smell of it is toasty and deep and rich, like fresh baked bread, or tobacco.

"I wanted to ask you something," I say. "The bug you gave me. Isn't it kind of late in the year? What happens when the butterfly comes out? If I let it go it'll freeze to death."

"You can keep it for an indoor pet," he says, grinning.

I taste my espresso. It hits the tip of my tongue and for the briefest instant it is sweet. Then it flows back into my mouth and I get hit with sour and bitter all at once. I swallow, and my mouth comes alive with intense coffee flavor even as my throat clenches, complaining of the potent bitterness. Guy is watching me; I keep my features carefully composed and wait a few seconds for my throat to loosen.

"It's good," I say, but Guy is looking over my head. I feel a presence close behind me and turn to look.

A tall, scrawny guy with short, shaggy hair is looking down at us. He has orange eyelashes. I think his hair would be orange too, if he didn't dye it black.

"Hey, Weevil," Guy says.

"How's it going, kid?" He extends his hand to me. "Hey there, baby bat. I don't know you, do I?"

"Not yet."

"Look at you. You're amazing."

I shake his thin, long-fingered hand. "Actually, I'm Lucy."

He laughs. "You're funny too. You a student at Harker?"

"At the moment I'm a future high school dropout."

"Really! A prescient future dropout. So, you guys going over to the Carfax tonight?"

"What's going on?" Guy asks.

"There's a thing. If you're not doing anything. You too, baby bat." He winks at me.

"Maybe we'll drop by," Guy says.

"You want a ride?"

"I got the dadmobile."

"Cool. See you there, Dilly." Weevil wanders off.

"Dilly?" I say.

Guy/Dylan/Dilly shrugs. "They used to call me that."

"Apparently, they still do."

"I like Dylan better."

"What about Guy?"

He grins. "I'm more used to Dylan."

"Okay. I'll call you Dylan. What's the Carfax?"

"The Carfax Arms. It's an apartment building over on the east side. The guy that lives there, Wayne, must be having a party. Interested?"

"What sort of party?"

"A goth thing, probably."

"I don't know. . . ." Sneaking out for a cappuccino was one thing. Driving across town to a goth party, that I wasn't so sure about.

"You're interested in vampires, right?" Dylan is grinning at me.

"So?"

"So maybe this is your chance to meet one."

15

Butterflies and Beer

The Carfax Arms is one of those old apartment buildings that was probably very chichi when it was built a hundred years ago, but now it's not so nice. The marble floor in the vestibule is cracked and stained, the brass mailboxes are tarnished to the color of mud, and the ceiling has been covered with the sort of cheesy acoustic tile you might see in a Kmart. The inner door is plain gray steel, cheap and forbidding.

There are only four mailboxes. The apartments must be huge, I think. Dylan presses the button under mailbox number four. The button is old and yellow and has the look of a buzzer that hasn't worked in twenty years. The name W. SMITH is printed on a piece of white tape beneath the button.

"Somebody'll come down to let us in," he says.

A minute passes. I can hear music and voices coming faintly from above. I'm too nervous to talk. A couple of times I almost ask Dylan to take me home, but it passes. Dylan has his hands in his pockets. I sense that he is not quite as cool and confident as he seems. Another minute passes. He presses the button again.

"I don't think it works, Dylan," I say.

The outer door opens. Three laughing black-haired girls crowd into the vestibule. Two of them I don't know, but the other one is Marquissa Smith-Valasco.

All three of them are wearing different perfumes. The clash of sweet and musk and spice is revolting.

"Hey, Dylan." Marquissa smiles brightly and touches her hair.

Dylan nods, still with his hands in his pockets.

Marquissa notices me. Her eyelids fall back to their usual half-closed position. "Lucy," she says.

"Good guess."

"What are you guys doing standing out here? Is the door locked?" She shoves the door and it opens. Marquissa and her friends push past us and start up the stairs, leaving a trail of scent. Marquissa looks back at us. "You guys coming, or what?"

We follow, feeling pretty stupid.

"Last time I was here the door was locked," Dylan says.

As we climb the stairs the smell of incense cuts through the perfume reek. The music gets louder. The lights in the stairwell are yellow. At the top of the stairs there is a landing not much bigger than the vestibule below. There are two doors. The one to the left has a steel bar across it with a large padlock. The other door, apartment number four, is painted purple. Or maybe it is maroon—it's hard to tell in the yellow light.

Marquissa and her friends walk right in. Dylan and I follow.

The first room is long and narrow. It looks like a stage set where the playwright has specified "ugly, gloomy, spooky, incredibly badly decorated room." A bank of windows along the right-hand wall is covered with heavy dark green brocade curtains. The floor is carpeted, and the furniture—a sofa and four big overstuffed chairs—is all draped with the same green brocade curtain fabric. At the far end of the room a small fire flickers in an oversize fireplace. The only other light comes from two matching brass lamps with opaque shades.

"Nice place," I say. Music is coming from farther back in the apartment, a throbbing, thumping, off-center beat.

Aside from us, there are only two people in the room: A guy and a girl sitting at one end of the sofa. I don't recognize them; they look older than us. Both are wearing the standard goth uniform: black, black, metal, red, black, metal, black, black. Standard Goth, of course, requires that each individual display at least one Very Unique (a redundancy, I know) Feature. In this case, the guy has a bolt through his lower lip. A nut is threaded onto the end of the bolt. It's probably not a real bolt, which would drag his lower lip down over his chin—not to mention the rust stains. I suspect it's a piece of hollow silver jewelry made to look like a bolt.

The girl's bid for uniqueness is orange stockings under her black leather mini. Orange is not one of the Approved Colors in the Official Goth Color Guide. It is a bold move, but not very attractive. (There are good reasons why orange didn't make the cut.)

On the table in front of them a spiral of smoke rises from an incense burner.

Marquissa and her crew walk right past them through a door leading farther back into the apartment.

"C'mon," Dylan says.

As we walk past the couple on the sofa I see that the fire in the fireplace is actually several candles, and that the boy is holding a beer mug full of something thick, dark, and blood red.

The apartment is like a maze. No, it's more like a series of interconnected stage sets, each one populated by a collection of weird actors. In one room we come upon four guys with shaved heads and enough hardware stuck in their faces, ears, and scalps to set off metal detectors for miles around. They look like soldiers from the same demon army. They are sitting on the floor playing cards and smoking cigarettes and laughing. They are probably in their twenties, although with all the hardware I can't be sure. Two of them are drinking the same blood-red concoction.

I grab Dylan's sleeve.

"What are they drinking?" I ask.

"Snakebite. Wayne must have a keg going. You thirsty?"

"No!" Again, I think that I should leave. But somehow I don't.

Marquissa and her friends have disappeared.

"C'mon." Dylan leads me deeper into the maze. We enter a smoky room where several goths are staring at a grainy black-and-white movie on an old-fashioned black-and-white TV set. The smoke reeks of cloves. The next room is the kitchen. Weevil is standing over a keg of beer. He fills his mug halfway, then opens a can of something—I can't read the label—and pours it into his beer. He notices us watching him.

"Hey there, baby bat," he says, blinking orange lashes. "Welcome to Waynesville." He takes another bottle from the counter, pulls the cork, and pours a shot of blood-red fluid into his mug. The beer turns dark. He takes a gulp and grins. His teeth are red.

My stomach wants to crawl up my throat.

He carries his mug back into the TV room.

I take a closer look at the bottles. The red stuff is raspberry cordial. The can contains hard apple cider.

"That was a pretty awful-looking drink."

Dylan is grinning at me. "It's called snakebite and black," he says. "You want one?"

I shake my head. But I do wonder what

it tastes like. I've had beer before. A few times. I actually don't mind it. I've had wine, too. My parents let me have a glass on special occasions. I can take it or leave it. Mostly I leave it. Alcohol has what Fish calls a "significant impact" on blood glucose. Besides, it clogs up my brain.

"Who is Wayne?" I ask.

"He lives here." Dylan finds a clean mug and pours himself a beer. He leaves out the cider and cordial.

"I'll have a sip," I hear myself say. I don't want him to think I'm a total prude.

He hands me the mug and I drink. A chain of bubbles gallops down my throat, bitter and sweet. Then I notice the butterfly on the knife.

At first I think it's a fake silk butterfly like you might see on a flower bouquet. But then it moves its orange and black wings, slowly. It is perched on the blade of a black-handled kitchen knife on the stained white Formica countertop next to half a lime. It feels wrong. What is a butterfly doing here, inside an apartment? On a knife blade? At night? In October?

I point at it.

"What?"

"The butterfly."

Dylan looks. "Oh. They're all over the place. Wayne raises 'em."

"He grows butterflies?"

"Where do you think I got you that chrysalis?"

The butterfly is slow-motion flapping.

"Does he let them go?"

"I guess they could fly out the window if they wanted."

"It's cold outside. It's October."

"They don't have to leave if they don't want to. C'mon." He takes my arm and guides me out of the ex-kitchen. We walk down a short hallway.

"How big is this place?" I ask.

"He's got the whole second floor."

The music is getting louder. We enter a large room with heavy brocade curtains and paisley wallpaper. About a dozen people, including Marquissa and her friends, are standing around smoking cigarettes, talking, and ignoring the three guys playing music. Actually, it's not really music. One of them, a big dopey-looking guy with huge hands, is slapping the fat strings of a bass guitar with his long fingers. Another one, smaller and sharp-featured, is holding a small drum between his knees, hitting it with his palms. The third musician is hunched over a violin, running a hairbrush up and down the strings. They all look drunk or stoned, and they sound like it.

I say in Dylan's ear, "They're really"—I search for the right word—"*dreadful*!"

He laughs, and we move to the next room. We are in a small library, bookshelves covering the walls. Bookcases are like magnets for me. I read some of the titles: *The Book of Lies* by Aleister Crowley, *The History of Witchcraft and Demonology* by Montague Summers, a collection of vampire books, and several titles by someone named James Branch Cabell. Whoever this Wayne is, he has interesting tastes in literature. I am reading the titles on the third shelf down when one of the books moves. I jerk back, startled, then realize that I am looking at another butterfly, this one sitting on the spine of a book titled *Practical Lepidoptery*.

Dylan touches my arm. I follow him down another short hallway and through a curtain made of heavy plastic strips.

We step into another world.

At least that's what it feels like. The heat and humidity and light hits me like a soft slap in the face. It takes me a moment to realize that we are surrounded by plants.

The room is long. I look up and see stars through a glass ceiling. We are in a greenhouse. The greenhouse is alive with butterflies. Butterflies in the air, butterflies on the leaves, butterflies everywhere.

Dylan leads me past a table covered with orchids, strange flowers with fleshy petals and leaves that look like the green skin of an extraterrestrial. I've never met an alien, but if I did meet one, they'd probably resemble an orchid. Along the glass wall is a long trough of dirt full of tall green weeds. The smell of plants—decay, fresh growth, and wet earth—is overwhelming.

At the far end of the room we come upon a black leather sofa, two matching chairs, and a long, low smoked-glass table. A man is sitting in one of the chairs with a glass of wine in his hand. He is looking down at the table and talking.

Across from him, on the sofa, sits a small, ghostly looking girl with black hair down to her waist. She is wearing a long black dress. Her legs are crossed, showing black fishnet stockings. Her thin white hands are draped over her top knee.

We stop outside the furniture circle.

"That's Wayne," Dylan whispers.

The man, Wayne, looks out of place. He is the first non-goth I have seen here. He has sandy, curly hair; a stubbly blond beard; and red cheeks. He is wearing a blue denim jacket over a Nike T-shirt. I think that he is about forty years old. His voice is very low, like the sound of boots scuffing through wet leaves. I can't quite hear what he is saying.

The girl is listening intently. A butterfly flits between them. Neither of them seem to notice. After another minute Wayne sits back and sips his wine. The girl nods, stands up, and walks past us as if we are transparent.

Wayne looks up, fixes his eyes upon me, and says, "Next victim?"

16

Wine Red

His red cheeks dimple like a little kid's. His teeth are small and short. I think if they were normal-size I might run, but those stumpy little teeth and red cheeks make him look harmless.

"Victim of what?" I ask.

"Your fate," he says, all serious. Now his voice is that of a priest: soft and pleasant and insidious. Then he laughs, deep and warm. He points to the sofa. "Have a seat!"

Dylan and I sit down.

"Who do we have here?" he asks, looking at me but talking to Dylan. His eyes are dark brown—so dark that I can't distinguish pupil from iris.

Dylan says, "This is Lucy."

"Ahhh!" He is looking at me so hard my skin feels hot. "My name is Wayne," he says. "I live here."

"It's very . . . nice," I say, trying to be polite.

"Be honest, now." He sips his wine.

I notice a large black and yellow striped caterpillar crawling across his knee. "You have a worm on your knee," I say.

Wayne gently removes the caterpillar from his knee, walks it over to the trough full of weeds, and sets it carefully on a leaf. "They eat only milkweed, you know." He watches the caterpillar hunch across the pale green leaf.

"Are you a professional butterfly rancher?"

He laughs. "It's just a hobby. Do you have any hobbies?" He sits down.

"Sometimes I pretend to be a high school student. I guess you could say that's my hobby."

"I suppose school takes up most of your time. You are at Seward High, yes?"

"How did you know that?"

"I like to keep track of all the young goths."

"I'm not goth."

"Of course you're not—no more than I—but you do share a certain fashion sensibility with them."

"I like black."

"It's a very practical color."

"Exactly."

"Is it interesting, pretending to be a student?"

"Rarely. Not that it makes any difference."

"What do you mean by that?"

"I mean, it doesn't matter how boring or not boring it is at school. At the end of the day I'm still myself."

Wayne's eyebrows go up. "That is very astute. We are all trapped that way, are we not?"

"Is that a rhetorical question, or are you looking for an answer?"

"You *are* intelligent. Would you care for a glass of wine?"

"No, thank you."

"A reading, perhaps?" He gestures at the table.

I look down at the deck of cards spread across the table. I've never before seen a real deck of tarot cards. They are slightly larger than regular playing cards. Each one has a colorful illustration. The scenes on them are quite strange—devils, magicians, bloody swords, and characters dressed in medieval clothing.

Wayne gathers the cards and slowly

mixes them together. "Looo-seee," he says, stretching my name out. "What shall we learn today about Looo-seee."

I feel my thighs tense. I am one second away from standing up and walking out of there when Wayne spills out his nice deep laugh and says, "I'm sorry! I should know better than to mess with people's names."

"That's okay," I say.

"No, it's not okay." He is serious again. "Names are important. Our names are who we are. You have a beautiful name. Lucinda. It means 'light'. Did you know that?"

I nod, surprised that he knows my full name. Most people would have guessed Lucille.

He turns up a card.

The card shows a man in a long black cloak standing before a river. Only a small part of his face is visible. His cheek is red. On the other side of the river is a small castle. Upstream, a bridge crosses the water. The sky is cold and gray. On the ground before the cloaked man, three tall golden cups lay on their sides. Two of the cups have spilled a red liquid onto the earth. The other cup has spilled something green. Behind the man are two more cups, upright, possibly empty, possibly full. I stare into the card, feeling almost as if I am there.

I hear a voice, very close. "The Five of Cups," he says. "Your card. Remarkable."

I look up. We are both leaning over the table, our faces only about a foot apart. His eyes are espresso and his breath has a sweet organic smell, like old apples.

"Why do you say that?" I ask, sitting back.

"It is a powerful card," he says. "You are a very special person."

"I bet you say that to everybody."

"Oh?" His grin makes him look like a little kid. "You are very astute, Lucinda. But in this case it is true. I surround myself with posers and pretenders. It gives me pleasure to have many friends. But you are different."

I look to my right, but Dylan is gone. The sounds of the party seem distant. I hear the thumping of a drum and a squeal of laughter.

"I don't have any friends."

"I very much doubt that, Lucinda. I am your friend, at least." Our eyes lock for a moment. "You are more powerful than you know. The world that surrounds you is what you make of it." He is looking into me. I drop my gaze to the table. The cloaked man is standing by the river, cold and alone. Wayne says, "The running water is a barrier he cannot cross. The spilled blood represents life; the green fluid is poison. He rejects the blood because he is ashamed. You see how the shame reddens his face? Yet he also rejects the poison for fear of death."

"Where did Dylan go?" I ask.

"He is probably enjoying the party. You aren't really a party person, are you?"

"I don't know what kind of person I am." I'm angry at Dylan for wandering off, but I don't really miss him. I'm not afraid. Wayne is a bit odd, but he seems harmless, and he understands some things. Still, I wonder why he surrounds himself with young goths.

He says, "Dylan has a great deal to learn about life. Things that you already know. He is a child."

"So am I."

"No." Shaking his head. "You are no child. You are very mature. You are more powerful than you know. I open my doors to many young people. I meet all kinds. Some older than me—and I am older than I look—have yet to grow up. Others are like you. You think about things. I can tell. Most people are sheep. They simply react to whatever life throws at them. You're different. Life reacts to *you*. You're a thinker, like the man in your card."

He taps the tarot card with his forefinger. "You see the castle? That is his home, to which he can never return. The bridge is his dream. The two upright cups represent false hopes."

Wayne turns up a new card.

A gray-cloaked, white-bearded man standing on a snow-covered mountaintop holding a lantern in one hand and a staff in the other. Inside the lantern, a star shines. "The Hermit," Wayne says. "My card. Like you, I enjoy the use of my intellect. I am a seeker of truth."

"Find any?"

He lifts his wineglass. *"In vino veritas,"* he says, and drinks. When he sees that I do not understand, he explains. "That's Latin. 'In wine lies truth.' Are you sure you wouldn't care for a glass? It's a very nice California pinot noir."

This time I say, "Okay."

He talks to me like an equal, an adult, an intelligent person who doesn't have to go to school or be home by eleven or check her blood sugar every three hours. I sip my wine. It puckers my mouth, bitter and sour, with the scent of berries and old wood, and a slight metallic tang. Not like the sweet, simple wine my parents drink on Thanksgiving and Christmas. I'm not sure I like it, but it's interesting.

"It's very good," I say and drink again.

"Yes it is. And may I say it is a pleasure to share a bottle of wine with one so lovely and intelligent."

"Thank you."

"You are always welcome here, Lucinda. Anytime. If you ever need a safe place to go, you are welcome. My doors are open. Shall we continue with your reading?"

The wine has pooled beneath my heart; I feel it burning. A butterfly lands on the edge of the table, then flits off. Wayne turns up another card.

A tall, gray tower on the top of a mountain is struck by a lightning bolt. The top of the tower, a golden crown, is blown off. Smoke and fire spill from the windows. A man and a woman are falling, surrounded by licks of flame.

"The tower," says Wayne.

I feel dizzy, as if I, too, am falling.

"Chaos, upheaval, revelation. A dangerous card, Lucinda."

I set my wineglass on the table. My arm seems longer than my body.

"Insight, crisis, eruption. You are entering into a period of great change."

I hug myself. I know that what he is saying is true. His hands grasp my shoulders and I am looking straight into his bottomless eyes.

"Promise me something, Lucinda. Promise me that if you need help, you will come to me."

I nod. His hands release me. I sit back, tingling where his hands gripped my shoulders. Everything is in sharp focus, as if someone has cranked up the contrast knob of reality. I stand up. I am ten feet tall.

"I have to go."

"Come back and see me," he says. "Come back anytime."

I lurch off, past the milkweed and the orchids, looking down at my feet, seeing flecks of black and orange on the wooden floor. I am scuffing through broken monarchs. The floor is littered with the dead.

I find Dylan talking to Marquissa.

"I have to go," I say, trying to make my voice hard. It comes out high-pitched and whiny. I don't care. He tries to argue with me, but I won't have it. I don't care about Marquissa and her sleepy, sleazy smirk. I don't care what any of them think. I have to get out. I half drag him to the door and down the stairs.

We get into his car.

"What's the matter with you?" he asks.

"I'm tired."

"Did something happen?"

"No." I feel so strange. "Why did you leave me with him?"

"He likes privacy when he does a tarot reading. That's his thing, the tarot cards. Pretty weird, huh?"

"He gave me a glass of wine."

"He must really like you."

Dylan's voice sounds far away. We are driving down a tunnel of streetlamps. When I blink, the lights move. Am I having an insulin reaction? Sometimes the symptoms are pretty peculiar. To be on the safe side, I dig into my purse for some candy. All I have is a bag of Gummi Bears. I shove a few in my mouth and force myself to chew and swallow.

"Gummi Bears?" Dylan asks.

"I'm hungry," I say.

"Oh."

For a moment I regret not telling him about my diabetes. But it's really none of his business. I get so bored with being Diabetes Girl, it's nice to have friends who don't think of me as a diseased cripple.

"I thought you were going to introduce me to a vampire," I say. It sounds like I'm talking from the bottom of a well.

Dylan looks over at me and says, "I did."

I slip in through the back door in my stockings, pad through the dark kitchen and up the stairs, feet whispering on the carpet. I can hear my father's snores and the sound of air passing in and out of my own lungs. I take a deep breath and open the door to my room, half expecting to find my mother sitting on my bed, waiting—but all is as before. No computer, clothes on the floor, rumpled bed waiting. I fall onto it. I should test my blood sugar. In just a few more seconds, I'll get up and prick my finger and squeeze out a drop of blood and make it be a number: 106, 34, 348. No number will surprise me. I feel the Gummi Bears swimming in wine soup, dissolving, sending glucose molecules through the walls of my small intestine. I see monarch wings crumbling.

Do I believe that Wayne Smith is really a butterfly-raising vampire? Not for a moment. Why would Dylan tell me such a thing? To impress me? He is such a child.

I close my eyes and see myself standing beside a river drinking nectar from a tall, golden cup. I see myself falling from a tower of stone. *Chaos, upheaval, revelation.* Wayne's words sounded familiar. Where have I heard them before?

"Chaos, upheaval, revelation," I say out loud. Who does it sound like? I try faces: My father, Mark Murphy, Dylan, Fish. . . . No one I know talks like that. I send my thoughts to books and movies, imagining the words in the mouths of actors and characters, but nothing rings true. I turn my thoughts to cyberspace and it hits me.

Draco. Draco used those words. Is it possible? Could tarot-card-reading Wayne actually be Draco the cybervamp? Did Dylan actually introduce me to a real vampire?

I roll myself up in my comforter enchilada style and tell myself that I am safe.

There are no vampires. Not anymore.

17

Fuzz

I rise as from death, my head thick with dream-goo, my body stiff with rigor mortis. What? What is it?

Knock knock knock.

I know the sound of my mother's knuckles.

Knock knock knock.

"Okay! Okay! Okay!" I shout. Or rather, I try to shout. It comes out as a pathetic gurgle.

"It's seven o'clock, Sweetie!" she says.

Seven o'clock. I have to be at school in forty-five minutes. I sit up. I don't feel so good. I still have my clothes on. My guts hurt. I imagine things growing inside me: Tumors, parasites, aliens.

"Sweetie?"

"Okay, I'm up!"

Footsteps recede; I flop back onto my pillow. I could skip school. Lie in bed all day and read. The thought of staying in bed gives me a warm moment, but I know it's not so easy. My mother would be in and out all day, fretting. *Honey/Sweetie/Sugar? Are you sure you don't want to see Dr. Fisher, Lucy Honey/Sweetie/Sugar?*

Better to head for school and sleep through classes, I think.

But I really don't feel so good. My head hurts and my face feels fat and my mouth tastes horrible, all sweet and sour. I stare up at the ceiling, at the Seven Sisters. The tiny dark spots are all fuzzy. So fuzzy that I can't even count them. I blink to get the sleep out of my eyes. No difference. I sit up and rub my eyes. Everything is out of focus. Can nearsightedness really come on that fast? Maybe I need glasses. Maybe I'm going blind.

I remember that I haven't checked my blood sugar since yesterday morning. Could I be having an insulin reaction? I find my meter in my coat pocket. I prick my finger and squeeze out a drop of red, then apply it to the sensor strip. The meter counts down, then beeps.

The display reads 494.

Four. Nine. Four.

For a moment I simply stare, confused. I have never before seen such a reading.

Four hundred ninety-four milligrams of glucose per deciliter of whole blood. Normal is more like 100, or 120. No wonder I feel like crap.

Fish says I should keep my morning blood sugars under 140.

"Is that what you do?" I ask.

"I try," Fish replies.

I wonder what he would say if he saw *this* number. Probably have me in the hospital in no time. I go into robot mode and get a fresh syringe and the bottle of fast-acting insulin from my purse. How much will I need to bring myself back to the land of the living? I have no idea, but I figure a lot. I load thirty units into the syringe, pinch up a mound of belly fat, and shove the needle all the way in. I depress the plunger.

There. Now all I have to do is wait for the insulin and the glucose to shake hands.

Still in robot mode, I motor down the hall to the bathroom and undress and climb into the shower.

Four ninety-four. How did it get so high? Did I forget an insulin injection? I try to remember my evening shot. I remember my dad waking me up, yelling at me. Then eating my mom's greasy potatoes . . . did I take my shot? Can't remember. Then drinking lattes at the Bean. Then the party—a sip of beer, a glass of wine . . . and on the way home, Gummi Bears. Even if I had remembered to take my shot before dinner, my blood sugar would have skyrocketed. What was I thinking going so long without testing? Especially after the wine and Gummi Bears. Stupid stupid stupid. I turn off the water and towel dry.

Stupid girl. What would Fish say?

"Lucy, you don't get another body. You only live once."

"I'm a Buddhist," I say. "We come back."

Fish shakes his head. "Lucy, Lucy, Lucy . . ."

Am I suffering from ketoacidosis? I try to remember the symptoms. Nausea, pain, vomiting, labored breathing, long sharp teeth, tremendous thirst, fear of crucifixes, eternal un-life . . .

Maybe my bottle of insulin went bad. I return to my room and do another blood test.

439.

That's good. It's coming down. The insulin is working. I check the clock. 7:21. Ten minutes to catch my bus. My life is ruled by digital displays.

I dress. Hmmm. Shall I wear black, or black?

I choose black.

As I am pulling on a pair of black jeans my eye catches the chrysalis hanging over my desk. I take a closer look. It's darker now, like the skin of a ripe avocado. I can see the shadow of striped wings through translucent green. The gold dots are brighter.

I think that something will be happening soon.

Going to school when I'm sick is a lot like going to school when I'm not. The major difference is that usually when Mr. BoreAss talks chemistry it makes my head go numb. Today, he makes my head pound. In fact, it feels like a bunch of insane, invisible dentists are drilling tiny holes in my skull, all of them making that dentist drill sound that is all Es:

EEEEeeEeEEeEeeeeeeeeEEEeEEEeeEE Eeeeeeeeeee EEEE . . .

"Lucy?"

I look up.

"Are you all right?" BoreAss's eyes are boring into me. What did I do? Was I making dentist-drill sounds? Have I turned into a bat? Did I remember to get dressed before I came to school? Everyone in the classroom is looking at me. I stand up, knocking my books to the floor. Something is horribly wrong. I don't know what it is but somehow I know I want a glass of orange juice worse than anything in the world. I step away from my desk and say, "I'm a little thirsty. . . ."

Then I am a cartoon coyote falling from a cliff, only instead of the bottom of a canyon, it is the linoleum floor rushing up at me.

18

Bad Girl

I rise from the dead in the nurse's office. My mouth is full of orange-flavored sweetness and Mrs. MacDougal, squinty-eyed and intense, is bending over me like a vampire about to enjoy a meal. I push her away and sit up. A knot of pain rattles my forehead. Everything is in hard and hurtful focus.

"Please lie down, Lucy," she says. "An ambulance is on the way."

"Don't need an ambulance. I'm okay." I wipe my chin with the back of my hand. It's all sticky.

"I'm afraid you've reacted to your medication," says Mrs. MacDougal. "I gave you some glucose syrup."

"It's called *hypoglycemia,*" I say. "No big

deal. I'm fine now." Except for my pounding head and a terminal case of embarrassment. Passing out in front of everybody. I knew I should have checked my blood sugar again before class. How many units did I take? Thirty? Too much, too much.

I want desperately to be at home, in bed, wrapped around my own pillow with my headphones on listening to Patti Smith or Johnette Napolitano, two women who know what it's like to be as pissed-off as I am.

"Please lie down. . . ."

"I'm fine, I told you." I stand up. MacDougal looks frightened. I *hate* it when people are afraid of my diabetes. She thinks I'll fall down in her office and she will be held responsible.

I hear a siren.

"No way I'm going to the hospital," I say, starting for the door.

Mrs. MacDougal grabs my wrist and gets in my face with her squinty eyes and tough-love voice. "Young lady, I want you to sit down right now. You've had a nasty fall, and you clearly do not have your diabetes under control. You are going to the hospital."

I jerk my arm away from her and push the door open and run down the hall.

"Lucy!" MacDougal calls after me but I ignore her.

Lockers like metal coffins line the empty hallway. If I keep moving my feet I will arrive at the front foyer. The glass doors will lead me out onto the street. The street will take me home. I am almost to the foyer when a rhinoceros appears before me. It is Gruber, the vice-principal, in his rhino-gray suit. He wears gray like I wear black. His arms are out, his legs bent, and his head is tucked down between his shoulders. Reliving his days as a high school football hero. Is he going to tackle me?

"Hold on there, Ms. Szabo," he says in his gravelly voice.

I dodge to the left but he is too quick for me; his right arm wraps my waist. I strike out, hitting him with my fists.

"Let me go you pervert!" I yell. He pins my arms to my sides. "Get your hands off me! Rape! Rape!" He scrunches up his face at my screaming but won't let go. "I'll sue! Help! Help!"

The hallway is filling with people. I see Dylan. I see Fiona Cassaday.

"Please calm down, Ms. Szabo," says Gruber.

I suck in a deep breath and shout, right in his stupid little ear, louder than I have ever shouted anything before.

"LET GO OF ME!"

Gruber shudders, but I am still his prisoner.

Of course, when they get me to the hospital all they do is give me about a thousand dollars' worth of tests I don't need then send me home and tell me to monitor my blood glucose more closely. Like I couldn't have figured *that* out . . .

My mother's knuckles are white on the steering wheel, and the windshield wipers are slapping back and forth, and the world is gray on gray.

So I had an insulin reaction. She should be used to it by now.

I'm never going to school again.

Talk about embarrassing. The whole school watching me wrestle with Gruber, screaming hysterically. The paramedics hauling me off. I'm sure they all think I've been institutionalized, wrapped in a straitjacket, locked in a padded room, doped up on lithium and Prozac. Maybe electroshocked and lobotomized, too. Actually, I think I'd rather have a lobotomy than go back to school.

My mother is talking. She talks a lot when she's ner- vous. I tune in to see what she's babbling about.

"—Rita Steiner said her daughter is

doing *so* well on her insulin pump. . . ."

I was afraid of this: Sandy Steiner's mom has gotten hold of my mother and they are plotting to hook me up to a machine.

"I'm not going bionic," I say.

She looks over at me. "Honey . . . ?"

Now she wants me to explain bionic. Forget about it. I slump deeper and stare out into the pouring rain.

19

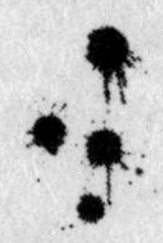

Shrink-Wrap

The shrink's bookshelves are full of toys and games. He has dolls and trucks and toy guns and robot action figures and board games and puzzles and a lot of things I don't recognize. I pick up something that looks like a Ping-Pong paddle with a hole in its center. I am looking at it when the door opens and Richard Carlson, M.D., steps in to the room.

He looks just like you would think: average in every way. I can't even tell how old he is. Somewhere between thirty and fifty. Sandy hair. Regular features. Average weight and height. He is wearing blue jeans to show me how casual and hip he is, and a tweed sport coat to show me he's a dork. He is holding a notebook with a green leather cover and a big friendly smile that didn't come with his face. I'm sure he practices it in front of a mirror.

"Hi," he says, extending his free hand. "I'm Dr. Rick."

He has a very soft, dry handshake.

"Lucy Szabo."

He looks at the paddle in my left hand. "Do you know what that is?" he asks.

"No." I put the paddle back on the bookshelf.

"Any guesses?" He is standing a little too close to me.

I back off a step. "It's a Ping-Pong paddle with a hole in it."

"And what do you suppose it's for?"

"Is this part of the evaluation?"

Dr. Rick laughs, a little too loud. "Just a question."

I do not like this Dr. Rick. "Why don't *you* tell *me* what it's for?"

"Tell you what. Why don't we sit down?" He directs me toward the two leather easy chairs.

"Which one is yours?" I ask.

"Take your pick."

"Why? So you can analyze my choice?"

"So that you'll be more comfortable. Are you uncomfortable?" His eyes are lit up. I sense that making patients uncomfortable is what he does best. He enjoys it.

I choose the chair that I think *he* prefers. I do not like this Dr. Rick. I am glad that there is a coffee table between us.

"So, Lucy," he says once we are settled. "I understand you've been having some problems at school."

"Actually, they've been having some problems with me."

He writes something in his green leather notebook. "Could you explain what you mean by that?"

I figure I should just cut to the heart of it. "Look, it wasn't my idea to come here. I'm getting some bad grades and I had an insulin reaction at school, I've got an English teacher with no sense of humor and a vice-principal who thinks he's still a football star. Other than that, everything is fine. No problem. The only reason I'm here is to get the brain police off my case."

Dr. Rick looks a bit startled. I've scored a point.

He says, "I hope you don't view me as one of the brain police."

I say nothing. Let him work it out for himself.

He clears his throat. "I think I understand something of why your teachers have been having trouble."

"What, I'm too surly and mouthy?"

"Lucy, I'm not going to beat around the bush with you."

"Good. I hate bush beaters."

"You're not a little kid anymore. You're making choices that will stay with you for a long, long time—"

BLAH BLAH BLAH.

"—so let me put it to you as directly as I know how. What happens in this room today, and on any future visits, is far more important to you than it is to me. I get paid either way. Whether or not this is a waste of your time is strictly up to you."

"Good," I say.

He gives me a couple seconds of his superior look, then nods crisply, as if he's won his point back. "All right then. You say your parents and teachers are having some problems with you. Is there anything you can do to help them?"

"Help them what?"

"With the difficulties they're having with your behavior."

"It's not my *behavior* that's bothering them. It's who I *am*."

"Everything they know about who you *are* is based on what you *do*."

This Dr. Rick has more moves than a spider monkey.

"Nobody wants you to change who you are, Lucy—"

"You're wrong about that."

"—but maybe you can make some adjustments that would make it easier for them."

"I could become invisible."

He smiles with his mouth but not his eyes, then sets his notebook aside and sits forward, leaning his tweed elbows on his denim knees. In a way he reminds me of Wayne the butterfly man—except that Wayne, for all his weirdness, never made me feel like a *subject*. This Dr. Rick just wants to *evaluate* me. He wants to take me apart, like I'm a machine.

"Anything on a more practical level?"

I don't say a word. I'm not opening any doors for this Dr. Rick.

He opens his notebook. "Let me ask you something, Lucy," he says as he makes a note. "What's the best possible result that you can imagine coming out of our meeting here today?"

I think for a moment. "I go home and you tell everybody that they should leave me alone."

He nods slowly. "All right. What's the second best possible result?"

"Giant asteroid crashes into Earth."

Dr. Rick sighs.

I almost feel sorry for him.

I refuse to talk to my mother about Dr. Rick.

"I'm sure he'll send you a complete report," I tell her. I go upstairs to my computerless room and shut the door. The chrysalis is getting darker. I don't know if it's dying or hatching. I kick off my boots and crawl into bed with a book I picked up at the library. The book is called *The Stranger*, by Albert Camus. I picked it because I like the title and it is very short and the author is French. *Was* French. I think he's dead. I'm on page two when I hear the doorbell ring. A few seconds later my mother calls my name.

I take a deep breath and shout, "WHAT?"

"Someone is here to see you," she shouts back.

"WHO?"

She doesn't answer. This can't be good. I untangle myself from the sheets and pull on my boots. One should never greet a mystery guest bootlessly. I hear voices from the kitchen. I head in that direction and find my mother pouring a glass of orange juice for Mark Murphy.

"Hey, Lucy," Mark says.

"Hey."

"Mark stopped by to see how you're feeling," my mother says. She likes Mark, a major strike against him.

"I'm feeling fine."

"Well then . . ." My mother is all twitchy. "I'll just . . . ah . . . I'll be downstairs. Folding laundry." She heads down the stairs.

Mark says, "I haven't seen you at school lately. You okay?"

My god, he actually *cares*. "Yeah, I'm okay. I mean, I'm not great, but I'm not sick or anything. I just needed to take some time off after . . . you know."

"After Gruber tackled you?" He's holding in a smile.

"Yeah."

"I thought you might take him. He's got a black eye."

"Really?"

"You nailed him." Mark is grinning now.

I grin right back at him. It feels weird the way it stretches my face. When was the last time I laughed? "I might come back to school just to see that."

Mark gets his serious look, the one that makes him older and more handsome. "So . . . you aren't officially suspended or anything?"

"No. They think I was having an insulin reaction. Temporary insanity."

"You weren't?"

"I had the insulin reaction earlier, in chemistry, by the time I ran into Gruber I was okay. I just wanted to get out of there. Don't ask me why."

"Why?"

"Well, it was kind of embarrassing, passing out in class. I don't know what I said. I might have said anything. I don't remember."

"I heard you just stood up and fell down."

"That's not so bad, then. Also, they wanted to send me to the hospital and I didn't want to go. I wasn't sick."

"Remember last time you were hospitalized?"

I think back. "That was a long time ago. I had a really bad insulin reaction."

"We were eight."

"We were playing some kind of game."

"Sleeping Beauty."

"I was in my princess phase."

"Yeah. We were in Little's Woods looking for dwarves or something, and all of a sudden you just curled up on the leaves and went to sleep. I couldn't wake you up." He is looking away, seeing into the past.

"So you went and got help."

Mark's face is flushed. I can't tell if he is embarrassed or angry or about to cry, and I can't understand why he would be any of those things.

"Not—I never told you this. I didn't go for help right away. I just watched you sleep. You were Sleeping Beauty."

"Really?" I remember Little's Woods, a two-acre patch of trees between the creek and the railroad tracks. A few years ago it was cut down to make room for another housing development, but when we were kids, Mark and I used it as our own private wilderness area. I imagine him watching me as I lay unconscious on the forest floor.

"Then I went home." He is really red now.

"To tell your mom?"

"I went home for lunch."

"You . . ." My mouth is hanging open. "You *left* me there in the woods?"

"I was just a little kid. I didn't *know*."

"I was in the hospital for *days*! Why are you *telling* me this?"

"I just had to. Look, I was thinking you were, you know, Sleeping Beauty. You could sleep for years. And I was *hungry*."

He looks so uncomfortable I feel a laugh spilling from my mouth. "Hungry? You're *always* hungry."

"I know," he says as if confessing to a terrible sin.

"How long did you wait before you told somebody where I was?"

"A couple of hours. Your mom came looking for you."

"So you told her where to find me."

"Not exactly. I knew everybody would get mad at me for just leaving you there, so I went back to the woods by myself. You were still asleep. . . ."

"More like in a coma."

"So I tried to wake you up, but you kept on sleeping. Then I remembered that there was only one way to wake up Sleeping Beauty. I kissed you."

"You did?"

"I . . . I'm sorry."

"For kissing me?"

"For being so stupid. For leaving you like that."

"Did it work?"

"What?"

"The kiss."

He shakes his head. I can almost feel the heat from his cheeks. "I had to run and get my mom. I never told anybody how long I'd left you there. Till now."

"That was a long time ago," I say.

"I still feel bad about it."

"We were just kids. Forget about it."

I see the muscles in his face relax. He

says, "You know what I think about sometimes? I imagine that I'm walking through the woods and I find you lying there, and I take you to the hospital."

"Why?"

"I guess to make up for before. I know it's really stupid, but I wish I could save your life sometime."

Okay, I think, this is a little too weird. My best friend, rock-solid Mark Murphy, is going off the deep end. Now I am embarrassed too. I wish I could give him something, a way for him to feel better about himself. Maybe I could ask him to do me a favor. Then I think of something.

"How late do you go to bed?" I ask.

"Pretty late."

"What are you doing tonight, say, around eleven?"

"Uh . . . I don't know."

"'Cause I was wondering if I could come over."

He stares back at me with such an utterly bewildered expression that I have to laugh.

20

Studying

Sblood: real world—where are you guys? what city?

Fangs666: Paris

2Tooth: Istanbul

Roxxxie: Ancient Babylon.

Sblood: SERIOUS! come on you guys! I realy have to know.

Fangs666: Fortress of Solitude

2Tooth: Mars City

Roxxxie: Ancient Babylon *SERIOUS* I'm logged on through a time link.

"I don't think they're gonna tell you," says Mark in a low voice. We are being mouse-quiet. His parents are asleep upstairs. We are in his room, way down in the basement, but his mom can hear hair growing, he says.

"I'm not surprised. Last thing most of them want is to meet a web friend face-to-face. Everybody knows we're all fat and ugly with questionable personal hygiene."

"I've been meaning to talk to you about that."

I swat his shoulder with the back of my hand. It's like hitting a stone wall. "Ouch," I say. "When did you get so Schwarzeneggery?"

Mark grins and rubs his shoulder. "I've been working out."

2Tooth: Y U wanna know?

Sblood: personal.

Mark says, "Why *do* you want to know?"

"I'm trying to figure out if this guy I met at a party is from our chat room."

"What guy?"

"An older guy."

Mark doesn't say anything for a few seconds. When I look at him he has this funny expression on his face. "You going out with him or something?" he asks.

"Me?" I have to laugh. "No!"

He looks relieved. For a second I don't get it, then I realize that Mark is jealous. Over *me*! And that makes me feel like I've got a lot of air in my chest. I breathe out.

"He's just this . . . kind of weird guy."

"Why didn't you ask him?"

"I don't know. Maybe I will if I ever see him again."

"But the people in the chat room could be anywhere, right? I mean, what are the chances they live here instead of a thousand miles away?"

"Pretty good, actually. Transylvania started off as an offshoot of a local goth Web site."

Sblood: anybody know where Draco's from?

2Tooth: N.

Roxxxie: Last we talked he said he was on a diet. No more blood from fat people. No more pig blood. Skinny girls and alleycat blood only.

Sblood: ever meet him F2F?

Roxxxie: NO WAY. I'm a skinny girl. He wants my blood he'll have to suck it out of me through my keyboard.

Fangs666: Tasty

2Tooth: I think he's from New Orleasn. He knows Anne Rice.

Roxxxie: Not New Orleans. I know all the Big Easy vamps.

Vlad714: What r you guys talking?

Sblood: Draco. Where he's from.

2Tooth: Why not ask him?

Sblood: He's not here. unless he's lurking. do you lurk, D?

"I'm not following this," says Mark. We are sitting next to each other in front of his computer. Our shoulders are touching.

"Draco is this so-called vampire that drops in on the chat room."

"I thought you were *all* vampires."

"Draco's more serious. All these guys *talk*

about drinking blood, but I think Draco might actually *do* it."

"That's pretty creepy."

"Not to a vampire."

Mark is looking at me. "This is a guy you think you met?"

"Maybe."

"Isn't that kind of scary?"

"A little," I admit. "But it's also kinda cool."

"What was he like? Did he look like Bela Lugosi?"

"Actually, he looked more like Elton John."

"Wow. That is scary."

I laugh out loud at the comical expression on Mark's face. He shushes me, pointing upstairs. That really sets me off; I clap my hands over my mouth and laugh through my nose, making a truly gross snorting sound, which gets Mark going too. A few seconds later we calm down just in time to hear footsteps from upstairs, followed by his mother's voice.

"Mark? Is that you down there?"

"Yeah."

"What on earth are you doing up at this hour?"

"Studying?"

There are three long silent seconds when

I imagine her standing at the top of the stairs trying to figure out if the snorting laughter she thought she heard was really the sound of her son studying. Just when I am sure she is about to march down the stairs she says, "Well, it's after midnight. Go to bed."

"Okay, Mom."

We listen to her shuffle back to her room.

"She's got ears like a bat," Mark whispers. His face is only about nine inches away from mine. He has little lines at the corners of his lips, and his eyes are the soft brown of chocolate pudding. His head is a planet, pulling at me. What would happen if I let go? If I let myself fall toward him and our lips smashed together? He kissed me once before, but I was in a coma. Not a very good kiss, at least from my point of view. I wonder if he is about to try again.

The thought sends a panicky jolt through my body. I stand up.

"I better go," I say.

I am standing on the street in front of Mark's house and my heart is going about a hundred beats a minute. Am I having another insulin reaction? I don't think so. I cut back on my long-acting insulin after the incident at school. If anything my sugar is a little high. I don't want to risk another bout of hypoglycemia, not after the last one. But why is my heart pounding?

I think about Mark's face, and our shoulders touching, and his chocolate-pudding eyes. I'm not breathing. I suck in a lungful of cool night air and tell my heart to slow down. It doesn't work. Going home and climbing into bed and sleeping seems impossible. I'm so awake right now my eyes feel like they're about to pop right out of my head. I should go back and make Mark talk to me. But I can't. Why not? I don't know. I start walking. Walking and thinking, thinking and walking, listening to the tock tock tock of boot heels on concrete.

I don't know where I'm going, but I'm sure I'll find out soon enough.

21

Adrift

It is 1:00 A.M. The Sacred Bean is quiet. No blue-lipsticked women playing music and only a handful of customers at the tables. I order a latte from a curly haired barista. Shall I take my latte with sugar, or aspartame? I wonder where my blood glucose is at. Probably high, since I've cut back on my insulin. On the other hand, I walked half an hour to get to the Bean. Just to be on the safe side, I stir in a couple of sugar packets. I carry my latte to a table in the back and open my book and read and sip and read some more.

The Stranger is about a man named Meursault whose mother dies, and he goes to her funeral but he just can't seem to get into it. It isn't real to him, or at least it isn't important. She's dead, so what's the point? He sits for hours by her coffin, which I guess you have to do in France, then finally he gets so bored he lights a cigarette, which you are not supposed to do even in France, but it turns out it's okay because the undertaker smokes too.

I wish I smoked. I would smoke right now if I had a cigarette. I would smoke a whole carton.

I look up from *The Stranger* and check out the other late-night caffeine fiends. The scene is not so goth tonight. There are a few black-leathery types, and a few college-student types, and one older college-professor type. That's fine with me. Even if Dylan were to show up, I'd probably ignore him. I go back to *The Stranger*. I know how he feels. I am on page twenty-three when I sense a presence. I stop reading, but I do not look up.

"Hey there, baby bat."

Now I look. It's Weevil, the tall, orange-eyelashed, snakebite-swilling goth.

"You all alone?" he asks.

"I have a book," I point out.

"Mind if I join you?" he asks, then sits without waiting for my answer. Tonight he is drinking espresso. He looks older than I remember. I'm guessing thirty. He holds his espresso delicately, pinching the handle between his long thumb and forefinger.

He says, "So how you doing?"

"Fine."

"Reading Camus?"

I nod.

"You ever listen to the Cure?"

I shake my head.

"They do a song about that book. It was on their first album." He sips his espresso. His lips are thin and flexible; they grip the rim of the cup like soft, flat fingers.

"How'd you get the name Weevil?" I ask.

He laughs. "My real name is Andy Anderson. Wouldn't *you* rather be called Weevil?"

"Do you go to Harker?"

"Not anymore."

"What do you do?"

"This and that. You and Dilly gonna be at the Carfax this Friday? It's Wayne's annual Halloween costume party."

"I haven't been invited."

"I'm inviting you now. I know he wants you to come. He likes you."

"I think he's a little old for me."

Weevil laughs. "*Everybody's* a little old for *you,* baby bat."

"Anyway, I don't have a costume."

"I bet you do. It's Bizarro Halloween.

Everybody comes dressed like a mundane."

He waits for me to respond, but I'm confused and say nothing.

"Look," Weevil says, "for us, life is a costume party three-hundred sixty-four days a year, right? So on Halloween, we cover up the tattoos, yank the piercings, and wear khakis and pastels. It's corduroys and penny loafers and sport coats and perky bows. It's Lands' End and the Gap and JCPenney and Sears. You must have something like that in your closet. Something your mother bought you." He drains the last of his espresso and stands up. "Dare to be square, baby bat," he says as he walks off.

The chrysalis is dark gray, a capsule of smoked glass. I think maybe it is dead. Looking closer, I see orange stripes and flecks of white, and I realize that I am seeing the monarch butterfly folded within a thin, transparent capsule. Most of the gold dots are still present, but one of them has turned bright blue.

I prick my finger to check myself for signs of life. My meter counts down, then delivers its pronouncement: 474.

Too high, too high, and I've had nothing but that one latte since dinner. In fact, I ate almost nothing for dinner—just a spoonful of rice casserole and a little salad. I inject a few units of insulin—not too much this time—and crawl into bed. The latte gave me a stomachache. Maybe I'm pregnant; a Virgin Vampire. Maybe I'm lactose intolerant. My mind is spinning and stuttering with coffee thoughts. The moon, nearly full, comes in through the window and bounces off my glass table, casting a milky light on the ceiling, lighting up Rubber Bat and the Seven Sisters. I wonder what they are saying.

Halcyone: Is that you, Electra?

Merope: Alas, Halcyone, 'tis but I.

Halcyone: Ah, the whine sister.

Asterope: Whine not!

Halcyone: What is this I see? A giant rubber bat?

Asterope: We are under attack! Where are our other sisters?

Merope: Lost forever, perhaps, for I cannot remember their names.

Sblood: It is I who cannot remember.

Asterope: An intruder! Who invited her?

Halcyone: Not I.

Merope: Nor I.

Electra: Nor I.

A chat room for the sisters.

I close my eyes and my thoughts swirl back to Mark Murphy. Maybe he would like to go to Wayne's Halloween party with me. The question then would be, since he always dresses like a mundane, would he have to dye his hair black and get his nose pierced? I smile in the dark, imagining it.

There was a time when I was maybe eleven or twelve when I had fantasies about marrying Mark. I would be a famous anthropologist, and he would be a professional golfer. We would travel all over the world together, exploring ancient ruins and winning golf tournaments. I don't know why, but I always imagined him with a mustache, and me with blond hair down to my waist.

Now, of course, the idea of Mark plus *moi* is way beyond the weird barrier. How would we look at the Seward prom? Mark smiling with his long wrists sticking out of a powder-blue rent-a-tux; me in funereal black and scowling. The photographer would crack a lens.

I look at my clock. Two thirty-four. Five hours until school starts. Am I going? I don't think so. The question is, how to negotiate it with the parentals. Maybe I pretend to be sick. Maybe I won't have to pretend. Maybe I'll wake up and my blood sugar will be some strange unheard-of digital mishmash, like $4.7\ \pi\ r^2/bc$. Or maybe I'll wake up dead, victim of a latte overdose. Or maybe a freak October blizzard will blow down from Canada and bury us all in nine-foot snow-drifts. Maybe the river will rise and flood the city. I see myself adrift on a river lined with lockers. My hand trails in water, soft and warm. I hear voices from the lockers as I pass: *Chaos. Disruption. Revelation. Eruption.*

I should just do what they tell me to do. Go to school. Be good. Do my homework. Be nice. Dress dorky. Eat meat. Act my age.

I could be an actress. Is that what Little Miss Perfect Diabetic Sandy Steiner does? Is she onstage 24/7? Maybe inside she's just as messed-up as me. Maybe she secretly thinks she should *be* like me. Ha. More likely she is a shape-shifter from the planet Dinglebat. I should take her to Wayne's. Tell her it's a diabetes seminar: Achieving Better Blood Glucose

Control Through Creative Bloodletting. All you need is a vampire with a sweet tooth for the ultimate in diabetes management. I see Sandy with her little insulin pump trying to be perky and cheery in a roomful of goths. I think of Weevil drinking snakebite, his smile red with raspberry cordial. The girl with orange stockings and the boy with the bolt through his nostril. Wayne and his butterflies. The sound of a hairbrush on violin strings. I wonder how Gruber looks with a black eye. Maybe I should invite him, too.

22

Angst

Have I ever had a morning when my mother's voice is not the first thing I hear? I bury my head in my pillow. Her strident tones slice right through the feathers and into my brain. I hold out as long as I can, then finally ooze over the edge of my mattress and insert myself into my bathrobe and shuffle out to the kitchen. My mother is making oatmeal. My father eats oatmeal every morning for his cholesterol. Then he eats great slabs of animal muscle for dinner. Go figure.

"I'm not going to school," I say.

"Aren't you feeling well, Sweetie?"

"I think I'm still recovering." In fact, I'm feeling kind of rotten. I had to get up to go to the bathroom about five times in the middle of the night. I wonder what my blood sugar is this morning.

"What's this?" My father enters, stage right. He is all suited up today. Big important meeting, no doubt. Going to sell some widgets to some dingbats. "No school?"

"Called off due to the plague of locusts," I say.

He actually looks out the window. No locusts. The corners of his mouth tuck in and he shakes his head. "Three days off is more than enough, Sport. Today you go to school."

"Seriously, I'm not feeling good."

He sits down before his steaming bowl of gruel. "No school; no computer."

I can tell from his voice and the way he won't meet my eyes that he has gone into his stubborn mode. Nothing I say or do now will change his mind. I could be having a seizure. I could be bleeding out of my eyeballs. I could have a knife jutting from my chest, and they'd still hustle me off to school.

I stomp up to my room to get my backpack. As I'm packing my insulin and syringe in my bag I try to remember whether I've taken my morning shot. I think back. I've given myself so many injections they all blur into each other. I'm pretty sure I already took it. I wouldn't want to give myself *two* injections—that would lead to another hallway tussle with Gruber.

I leave the house in a miserable black cloud. I don't even bother to test my blood. I really *am* sick, I think, whether they believe me or not. There must be *something* wrong with me.

At school everybody ignores me, like I never passed out in class or punched out the vice-principal. BoreAss is still prattling on about acids and bases and everybody is staring through him with varying degrees of incomprehension and no one seems to remember that seventy-two hours ago I disturbed their mundane reality with my hypoglycemic event. Maybe I'll have another one, just to liven things up.

Forget it. I'm too tired and cranky to pass out.

Nobody says a word to me till the next class when Dylan—excuse me, *Guy*—sidles up to me and says, "*Ça va?*"

"*Ça va* yourself. I'm not talking to you." Actually, I'm glad to have somebody to take my crankiness out on.

"Why not?" He is smiling but his brow is wrinkled, like he's not sure if maybe he did something.

"Two reasons. One, you left me all alone with a vampire. He could've sucked the life out of me."

"That's just—look, you don't really believe that stuff."

"The other reason is you didn't call me after . . . after I ran into Gruber. I could've been dead."

"I heard you were okay."

"Oh yeah? From who?"

"I don't know. Everybody. I mean, if you were really sick we'd all know about it, right?"

"You didn't call," I say.

"Sorry."

"I probably wouldn't have talked to you anyways."

"Oh. So, how come you never told me you had diabetes?"

"Because it was none of your business, maybe?"

"Does that mean you're not interested in going to a Halloween party tonight?"

"Why? Because you think I shouldn't eat candy?"

"How come you're so mad?"

"Now you think I'm crazy?"

"I didn't mean—"

"My diabetes doesn't make me a freak."

"I don't think you're a freak." He is looking right at me with those blue eyes.

"Good," I say.

"So, you want to go to a costume party?"

"The bizarro costume party at Wayne's?"

"You heard about it?" He is surprised.

"Weevil invited me."

"Weevil?" He is *very* surprised.

"But I'm not going. I have to be on my best behavior or the parentals might stick me in an institution for angst-ridden teens."

"Really?"

"I'm not talking to you."

Angst is my word of the day. Yesterday I overheard my father use the term "teenage angst," presumably referring to me, so I looked it up. *Angst* describes a feeling of anxiety, apprehension, anger, foreboding, depression. There is probably a tarot card for *angst*. I can even use it in a sentence: I am feeling very *angstish* in the face of Dr. Rick's professional cheeriness.

He seems to have turned up the wattage on his manufactured smile. I must not have been clear with him last time. Cheerfulness does not play well here in Lucyland, where we take our *angst* seriously.

"I hear you've returned to school, Lucy."

"In a manner of speaking. I attended all of my classes today. But please don't ask me what I learned."

"All right, you've got a deal."

"My father has promised to return my computer to me if I do okay in school the next few weeks. And stay away from scary chat rooms. And visit you."

"Will you be able to do that?"

"What choice do I have?"

Dr. Rick makes a note. I suspect that he isn't actually writing anything in that green notebook. He's just trying to look busy. I have used a similar technique in school.

"What are you writing?" I ask.

"Just making a notation."

"What does it say?"

"It's a note to myself."

"Can I see it?"

Dr. Rick closes his notebook and goes stern. "Lucy, why are you here?"

"Because I wrote an essay that my teacher didn't like."

He smiles. "The one about the vampire? I thought it was quite good," he says.

Now I'm *really* surprised. It's the first thing Dr. Rick has said to make me think he's not completely brain-dead.

"Well," I say, "you're in the minority."

"You're a very intelligent young woman. No one doubts that. Your theory about the origin of the vampire legend is quite provocative. And disturbing."

"That's me. Provocative and disturbing."

"Some people have a lot of trouble with that."

"They should get a life."

"*They* aren't going to change, Lucy."

"So what am I supposed to do? Dress up like Cathy Cheerleader and write a stupid essay about how I want to be an airline stewardess?"

"Do you want to be an airline stewardess?"

"Not particularly."

"Do you ever wonder why you're so angry?"

That sets me back. Not because it's a brilliant, insightful question, but because it is just so completely lame and manipulative. In the first place, I'm not angry. If he wants *angry* he should go talk to suicide bombers and road ragers and losing basketball coaches and irate vice-principals. In the second place, what's not to be angry about? I can't think of one good thing that's happened to me lately. But I'm not really angry. Pissed off, maybe, but not *angry*. If I ever get *angry*, you better watch out.

"No," I say. "I never think about it."

"Are you angry about your diabetes?"

"I'd rather not have it, if that's what you mean."

He writes again in his notebook. What a jerk.

❧

After Dr. Rick, I'm completely exhausted and more pissed off than ever. I only had about five hours of sleep last night, but it feels like I had none. I should take my crankiness home and put it to bed, but my feet decide to head over to Antoinette's. They want me to change? I'll show them change. I have in mind something black and red and spiky and depraved. A tattoo of a heart being shredded by a buzz saw, or maybe a pair of permanent fang marks on my throat.

By the time I get there the temperature has dropped and I'm cold. I spend a few minutes looking at the window display. I am considering a design based on an old Revolutionary War flag, a coiled snake with the words *Don't Tread on Me,* when the door opens and Antoinette steps out and fires up a cigar.

"Hey girl," she says in her ragged voice. She looks up at the gray sky. "Looks like winter's coming on Halloween this year."

"I guess."

"Still shopping for your first tat?"

"It's a big decision. They still don't wash off."

"That's what's so good about 'em."

I look at her arms, at the dozens of tiny black crosses, the flaming skull, the red heart, and the other symbols, images, and messages.

"Don't you ever wish you could erase any of them?"

"Every day, girl."

"Oh." I wait a couple seconds to see if she'll tell me which ones she regrets, but Antoinette just stands smoking and looking up at the sky.

"I have a question," I say. "What's the difference between pissed off and angry?"

"Pissed off doesn't last as long. Why do you ask?"

"Just curious."

She gives me an Antoinette laser look. "Something going on with you, kid?"

"Well . . . you know a lot of different kinds of people, right?"

She laughs. Antoinette's laugh sounds like a motorcycle starting up. "You could say that. Why?"

"You know a guy named Wayne?"

"I know lots of Waynes."

"This one raises butterflies."

"Oh *that* Wayne. I shoulda known. You been hanging out with him?"

"I wouldn't exactly call it 'hanging out.'"

"Whatever, girl. You know, I've got a special tattoo for girls who party with Butterfly Wayne. You want to see it?"

I shrug, curious. Antoinette pulls a pad of paper from the breast pocket of her vest.

She writes something on it, then turns the pad to show me. The page contains one word: STUPID

The chrysalis is collapsed and wrinkled and black, hanging off my shelf like a dead cigar ash. I stare at it and feel an empty dark space forming in my gut. Did I do something wrong? Is my room too hot? Too cold? Did I kill it by carrying it in my pocket for two days?

I hear Wayne's voice in my head. He is saying, *You are more powerful than you know. The world that surrounds you is what you make it.*

Did I make the butterfly die?

I sit on the edge of my bed. My face is hot and my belly aches. I'm bone-tired but my head is full of thoughts. Am I having an insulin reaction? I am fumbling for my meter when something warm spills down my cheek and I realize I am crying. How stupid. Crying for a butterfly. I drag my sleeve across my eyes. Crying for a bug. I flop back on the mattress and feel something crumple beneath me. I sit up and look back and see an envelope on my bed.

It's a normal-size white envelope with my name and address neatly printed in block letters. No return address. I tear it open. A smaller black envelope falls out. I pick it up and turn it over. Across the front of the black envelope, in red script letters, is printed the name *Sweetblood.*

But nobody in the real world knows I'm Sweetblood. Nobody except Mark, that is, and he's not a black-envelope type of guy.

I open the black envelope. Inside is a piece of black stationery. I unfold it and read the red-lettered words:

Dare to Be Square
9 p.m. until ???
Carfax

A shudder runs up my spine. I imagine a dark figure materializing beside my bed, placing the envelope there for me to find. I look around, but I am alone. I look up.

Rubber Bat hovers a few feet above my head. On his left wing sits another creature exercising its bright orange and black wings..

"Hello, Mr. Monarch," I say. I stand on the bed and reach out, offering it my finger as a perch. The butterfly launches itself, avoiding my finger. It circles Bat, then heads for the window, landing lightly on the sill.

Outside it is raining and cold. Not good butterfly weather.

"What am I going to do with you?" I ask.
Mr. Monarch refuses to speak.
"I suppose you'll be getting hungry."
Wings flap slowly.

23

Trick or Treat

"I thought you weren't talking to me."

"I'm not. But I need a ride to Wayne's." I am on the phone in my father's den, far from motherly ears.

"What am I, your ride boy?"

"It's an emergency."

"Yeah, right. Since when is going to a costume party an emergency?"

"It's life or death." Life or death for Mr. Monarch, that is. Wayne's greenhouse is his only hope to make it through the winter.

"Yeah, right. Are you gonna be mean to me all night?"

"Maybe. What are you wearing?"

"White Hush Puppies and stone-washed blue jeans."

"That's intense."

"Wait till you see my shirt."

"What time are you going? I'm still kind of grounded. I'll have to sneak out."

"I still haven't said you could come."

"Oh. Can I? *S'il vous plaît?"*

Dylan makes me wait about two seconds before he says, *"Oui."*

"Mom? Remember that sweater you got me last Christmas? The one with the heart? You know where that is?"

She looks up from her potato peeling, startled. "I put it in the box of clothes for the Goodwill. I thought you didn't like it." My mother should know better than to buy me clothes.

"Where's that?"

"In the basement, Honey."

I start for the basement stairs.

"Honey? Did you see the letter I left on your bed?"

I stop. "You put that there?"

"Well, yes. How else would it have gotten there?"

"I don't know."

"What was it? There was no return address."

"It was *personal.*"

"Oh." Her face pinches together and she

turns back to her potatoes. I head down the stairs.

I find the sweater beneath a pile of my father's old suits. Back in my room, I assemble my outfit. I check out my reflection. The sweater is black, which shows that she was trying to buy me something in my color, but it has an enormous appliqué on the chest: a huge red heart with a white lace border. Gee, thanks Mom. It goes nauseatingly well with my tan corduroy slacks and two-tone cowboy boots. Actually, the chocolate-and-cream boots are pretty cool. They were one of the last things I bought before I became seduced by the dark side. I should go to school like this. No makeup, hair in pigtails, dorky outfit—they'd love me. I'd probably get automatic straight As. I go downstairs to put my costume to the ultimate test. My mother is poking a fork at something in a fry pan.

"Hi Mom," I say.

She looks at me and almost drops her fork. "Lucy! You look . . . nice!"

Perfect. "Thanks!" I peer at the two sizzling things in the pan. "What's cooking?"

"Braised pork chops." Pig muscle, my father's favorite. "You don't want one, do you? I have more in the freezer. . . ."

"No thanks. I've had my pig quota for

this lifetime." The thought of eating flesh makes my stomach do a flip-flop.

"I'm making scalloped potatoes and lima beans, too." Going the extra mile for her scary diabetic daughter. If I wasn't there they'd probably eat nothing but pig.

"That'll be great, Mom." I look at the clock: 6:13. Five hours and two minutes till the Great Escape.

Dinner comes off without a hitch. The pig muscle is consumed. I manage to get down a few bites of salad and potatoes, even though I feel kind of nauseous. I don't know if it's nerves or what. Maybe it's my outfit that's making me sick. My father keeps looking at me like he can't quite believe that this is his daughter, but he never says a word about my new look. Maybe he thinks I am making fun of him, or maybe he actually likes it. For all its simplicity, the parental mind is beyond my understanding. We are just about done eating when the phone rings. I jump up and answer it before they remember to invoke the phone ban. It's Dylan.

"I have a serious problem," he says.

"Is it terminal?" I ask.

"Worse. I might not be able to go to the party tonight."

"Oh." I take the phone into the hall. "I

wasn't really planning on going anyway," I say. "Got to do the parentals proud. I'm kind of on a roll." I'd been good little SweetieHoneySugar all week. Mr. Butterfly can wait one more day. I think.

"My problem is that all my jackets are black," Dylan says.

"Ah, I understand." Maybe I will go to the party after all. "You are too cool."

"They don't go with my outfit. I'd skip the jacket, but it's supposed to be cold tonight."

"It's freezing out already." The rain had turned to sleet. Not a good night for the trick-or-treaters.

"I suppose I could just wear one of my dad's overcoats."

"Maybe . . . hey! I got an idea."

"What?"

"It's a surprise."

As soon as I get Dylan off the phone I call Mark.

"Is this Monkey Schwarzenegger?"

"Is this Skeeter McBee?"

"Speaking."

"Speaking."

"Thank God we got that over with."

"What's up? You trick-or-treating tonight?"

"Oh yeah, I got my little magic princess

costume on. Actually, I'm calling to ask a favor."

"Sure."

"Only you can't ask me why."

"Why?"

"Because if you do I'll lie."

"Really?"

"Really."

He hesitates, but I know he'll say yes.

The parentals are nothing if not predictable. At 11:00 the television set goes off, then ten minutes of bathroom noises and they are in dreamland. I catch the sleepy, hungry monarch and put it in a shoebox. An old red down ski jacket completes my dork ensemble. I grab my purse and take a last look at myself in the mirror.

"Lucy?" I ask.

The figure in the mirror nods. I take a quick look around. I have a feeling I'm forgetting something. Oh yeah. My glucose meter is staring at me from my desk. Got to check the old blood sugar. Got to be diabetes girl. I think of all the numbers the meter might shout, and none of them appeal to me. Besides, I'm tired of all the finger pricks and blood drops and digital numbers.

I turn my back on the meter and head out. I don't think I can climb down the antenna post holding onto the shoebox, so I tip-toe down the stairs and slide out through the back door quiet as a bat. It's sleeting out, more ice than rain. I run up the street, ice pellets chattering on nylon and stinging my face. Dylan is waiting at the corner all toasty warm and dry in his daddy's car. He is wearing the stone-washed jeans, as promised, and a black T-shirt with a screen-printed front.

"Is that my dork jacket?" he asks, looking at my puffy red cocoon.

"As a matter of fact, no, this is *my* dork jacket. What's your shirt say?"

He turns so that I can see the words: *Neil Diamond 1987 World Tour*.

"That is so uncool," I say with sincere admiration and disgust.

"What's in the box?"

"The reason I have to go to Wayne's."

He looks puzzled.

"You should know. It's all your fault."

"What did I do?"

"You gave me a butterfly."

"Oh. It hatched?"

"You could say that."

"Well, it wasn't from me, really. It was from Wayne."

"It was?" This gives me a peculiar and not altogether comfortable feeling.

"What about my jacket?" Dylan asks.

"Turn around and drive back down Oak Street."

A few seconds later I say, "Pull over here." I jump out and run across the lawn, the heels of my cowboy boots going *squish squish squish* in the soggy grass. I run around the house, down into the backyard where I knock on the door to the walk-out basement.

"Trick or treat," I say when the door opens.

Wordlessly, Mark Murphy hands me his letter jacket.

24

Bizarro

Dylan loves it. "This is so beyond uncool it's cool." He admires his reflection in the glass door of the lobby. The jacket is so big on him the sleeves hang past the tips of his fingers. "Look at me, I'm a football star."

"Be nice," I tell him. "It belongs to a good friend of mine."

"Problem is, it covers up Neil Diamond."

"So wear it awhile, then take it off." We start up the stairs.

"I could just sort of hang it off my shoulder."

"Yes, *très élégant*." We hear voices as we approach the landing. The door to Wayne's apartment is cocked open; the reek of clove cigarettes carves into my nostrils. We enter and find ourselves in a ghost world of abnormal ordinaries. One of the first people I see is a smiling, fresh-faced young man with carefully combed blond hair, a heather gray sweatshirt with GOD LOVES YOU! printed across the front, cargo shorts, and hiking boots.

"Greetings!" he says, and gives us both a vigorous handshake. "What a great day! Praise the Lord!"

There is a moment when I almost believe I have wandered into a Lutheran day camp—then I recognize him.

"Weevil?"

"No ma'am, my name is Andy Anderson. And may I say you look smashing in your puffy red coat? And you, sir—an accomplished athlete, no doubt?"

"Jeez, Weev, that's really scary," Dylan says. "Love the shorts."

"Enjoy! Enjoy!"

Andy/Weevil greets the next pair of guests, a couple dressed in Banana Republic khakis. Dylan and I weave through the maze of rooms to the kitchen, where two girls wearing matching pleated skirts and fluffy sweaters are serving hot apple cider in Styrofoam cups. We each take one. Maybe it will settle my stomach.

Most of the people there are very

strange-looking. Nobody is wearing anything that would excite comment in the mundane universe. The outfits are mostly what you might see on a Saturday afternoon at the mall. But none of it looks quite right. If alien invaders land and try to blend in using the Sears catalog as a reference manual, they might look something like this. For one thing, almost everybody has black hair. A lot of them are showing tattoos, and a close look reveals various punctures and indentations—evidence of piercings not currently in use. Then there is the way they move. Everybody is kind of stiff and tentative, and I know how they feel. I, in my corduroys and cowboy boots, am as uncomfortable as the rest of them. I feel naked without my makeup.

The strangest thing of all is the way everybody keeps *smiling*. And *laughing*. But their smiles and laughs do not have a happy, relaxed sound. They are more like the coughs and twitches and grimaces of discomfort, embarrassment, confusion, awkwardness.

Someone puts a Celine Dion CD on the stereo. It's the perfect choice—she's an alien in disguise too—but I'm not sure I'll be able to stand it. I take a sip of my cider. It's very odd-tasting.

"What is this?" I ask Dylan.

"I think it's hard cider," he says. "It's got alcohol in it."

"I don't want to get drunk."

"Then don't drink it."

"I'm really thirsty."

"Maybe there's some soda or something—hey, is that Marquissa?"

It is. Marquissa wearing a baseball cap. Her hair, gathered into a ponytail, is strung through the back of the cap. It gives her an uncharacteristically perky, long-necked look. Standing beside her, smoking a cigarette, is Fiona Cassaday, wearing a Seward Stingers cheerleader's sweater. The funny thing is that last year Fiona actually *was* a cheerleader.

"Hi guys," I say.

Marquissa gives me her usual heavy-lidded look. Some things never change. But I get a double take from Fiona.

"Oh my *god*!" she says, eyes wide. "Is that *you*, Lucy?"

"Tonight you can call me Lucille," I say. I take another sip of my cider. It tastes pretty good.

Fiona grabs my arm and pulls me aside. "Do you *know* these people? Have you *been* here before?"

"Sure," I say as if I've been there a thousand times.

"This is so *peculiar,*" Fiona says, eyes darting. "Marquissa's been trying to get me to come here *forever.* Look at how *weird* everybody's *dressed.*"

"It's a costume party, Fiona."

"*I* know *that.* I even dug out my cheerleader sweater. Hey, what's in the *box*?"

I'd forgotten I was carrying it. "A present for our host."

"Was *I* supposed to bring one?"

"No. Just me."

"I hear he's really *weird.*"

"Actually, the weirdest thing is how normal he is."

The second I say that, a creature in black glides into the room and all conversation comes to a halt.

At first I think, This guy didn't get the message about the costume party. He is wearing a flowing black cape over a black leather corset and black leggings. His lips are painted red, his hair is black and oily and combed straight back, his face and hands are pale with foundation: a caricature of a Hollywood vampire.

"Good evening, my children," he says. The voice is familiar . . . then I see who it is under all that makeup and everything makes perfect sense.

After all, this is Bizarro Halloween.

All of us black-clad freaks are dressed as mundanes, why shouldn't Denim Jacket/Nike T-shirt Wayne Smith dress up all vampy? Actually, he doesn't look half bad. The leather corset is a little silly, but I suppose he needs it to hold his belly in. Maybe I should get one for my dad.

"You *are* a spooky-looking bunch," Wayne says, putting his hands on his hips. I look down and notice his high- heeled boots. No wonder he looks taller.

"Hey, Wayne," I say.

He snaps his head around and fixes his eyes upon me. "Did I hear a peep?"

I give him a little finger wave.

"Ah," he says. "The raven-haired mundane speaks a strange name. Who is this 'Wayne' you speak of?"

Now I'm confused. Maybe this *isn't* Wayne. I don't know what to say, so I shrug.

He walks over to me and looks into my eyes. "Allow me to introduce myself, child." He holds out a red-nailed hand. "Draconius Mundo." He bows and plants a kiss on the back of my hand, then looks up at me. Lips curl back from stumpy little teeth, and he winks. Definitely Wayne.

He releases my hand and spins, his cape billowing. "Cider in the kitchen, children. Wine in the study."

Wayne, aka Draconius, does another cape-swirl and stalks off.

Fiona says, "Was that *him*? I thought you said he was *normal*."

"This is Bizarro Halloween. Everything is backwards."

"Well I think he's *creepy*." She follows Marquissa out of the room.

I search for Dylan and find him sitting on a sofa eating potato chips and slurping hot cider and listening to a girl dressed in a ruffled powder-blue blouse and a matching pleated skirt. Last time I saw her she was in fishnet and vinyl.

"What did you mean before, about Wayne giving me the chrysalis?" I say, interrupting her.

Dylan looks up with a mouthful of chips. "Huh?"

The girl has a nasty little smirk. I'd give her a black eye like I gave Gruber, only I'm afraid it would look good on her.

I say, "You told me in the car that this"—I'm still holding the shoebox with the butterfly—"was from Wayne."

Dylan gulps his cider. "Oh. He told me to give it to you."

"But he didn't even know me then."

"He knew who you were."

This sends a shiver up my spine. "How did he know that?"

"How should I know? Why don't you ask him?"

I stare at Dylan with new eyes. He looks small and young and weak. Mark's Seward Stingers letter jacket is huge on him. I can see why they call him Dilly.

"What are you, his message boy? That's really pathetic."

"What-*ever*." He shrugs and drinks more cider and the jacket sleeve slides back to reveal his wrist. The hilt of his tattooed sword is missing.

"What happened to your tattoo?" I ask.

"Umm, I guess it's coming off."

"It's fake?" I feel betrayed, as if he has lied to me. "That's so . . . high school."

"I'm thinking about getting a real one."

I turn away and head for another room, any room. I am half furious and 100 percent paranoid. Are Butterfly Rancher Wayne and Chat Room Draco the same person? Coincidences happen, and the whole goth/cybervamp community just isn't that big . . . but somehow he found out that Sweetblood was Lucy Szabo. The chat room was supposed to be anonymous. It was supposed to be safe. How had he found me? And why?

25

Wine and Chocolate

I don't like it when people play games with me. I don't put up with it from parents, or teachers, or anybody else. The more I think about the game this Wayne/Draconius/Draco is playing, the madder I get. Is he trying to frighten me? I'm not a scared little girl. I can take care of myself.

Part of me wants to confront him, but I know that's not a good idea. I should leave. I don't feel so good. Maybe I have the flu. My head hurts and my throat is tight and my stomach feels like it's full of lead. I should make Dylan drive me home. Now, before he gets drunk.

But I still have the butterfly box in my hands. I still have to let the poor thing go. I lift the lid and peek inside; the monarch is sitting quietly on its bed of crumpled tissue. I find the short hallway that leads to the greenhouse. Pushing through the plastic curtain, I am once again surrounded by the smell of moist earth and rotting vegetation, and the flickering of fluorescent tubes. This is where my butterfly needs to be, among the milkweed and flowers and warmth. I set the box on a long table crowded with orchids and remove the lid. The butterfly does not move. Is it okay? Should I lift it out of the box? I reach for it, and suddenly it is airborne, flitting toward the glass ceiling.

"You are returning my gift?"

I jump and let out a yelp.

He is standing a few feet away, partially hidden behind the milkweed plants.

"Don't sneak up on me like that!"

Draconius/Wayne moves into the light. "Sneak up on you? I was standing here when you walked in."

"You scared me."

"I was waiting for you."

"To scare me?"

"Hardly. I wish to apologize."

"Oh." That was about the last thing I expected. "For what?"

"For deceiving you. Come, join me." He heads back toward the sitting area where, just a few days ago, he read my tarot cards. It seems like months. I follow him. "I'm afraid I haven't been completely honest with you, Lucy. You deserve better."

A bottle of wine and two glasses are sitting on the glass table.

"Would you care for a glass of port?" he asks. The fluorescents give his makeup a greenish tinge.

"No, thank you."

"You've come all this way, and you won't let me share a drink with you?"

"I have to go home."

"Do you want to go home?"

Do I? Home to my empty desk and shred of chrysalis? I open my mouth to reply, but nothing comes out.

Draconius/Wayne smiles and pours two glasses half full of deep red wine and hands one to me. He sits down on the leather sofa and pats the cushion beside him. "Have a seat."

I would rather sit in the opposite chair with the table between us, but he is looking at me with those dark brown eyes and smiling, and he is apologizing to me, and it seems unspeakably rude—rude even for me—to refuse to sit next to him. So I do.

"Are you having a good time?" he asks.

"Not really." I taste the port. It is sweet and thick.

"Don't you enjoy seeing people's shadow selves?"

"I think I'm seeing them as their dorkoid selves."

Wayne/Draconius laughs. I take a larger sip of the port. It feels good going down. My stomach likes it.

I say, "What about you? What are we supposed to call you?"

"Tonight? Tonight I am Draconius. Tomorrow I'll be just plain Wayne." His smile is sad—or as sad as it can be, with all that red lipstick.

"What about Draco?"

"Ah, Draco." His hand pats me on the knee, then pulls back before I can object. "Draco lives in cyberspace."

I shift a few inches away from him. "So you *are* Draco."

"At times." He sips his wine, then wrinkles his nose. "This lipstick makes everything taste awful. I don't know how you girls can stand it."

"You get used to it," I say.

"*You* look good without it. You are a very attractive young woman, Lucy."

I try to let that comment roll off me, but some of it sticks. "So what's the deal with all the names?" I ask. "What's your real name?"

"I have many names."

"What's the name on your birth certificate? Is it really Wayne?"

"I don't remember. I was very young then."

"I think I like you better as Wayne."

He laughs. "I thought you were into vampires. You certainly spend enough time in the Transylvania chat room."

"On-line is different."

"Is it?"

"Do you really drink pig blood?"

He holds his wineglass up to the light. "But of course!" he says, deepening his voice.

I set my glass on the table. "That is so gross."

"I'm only kidding," he says. "None of this is real, you know."

"I'm real."

"I'm talking about the poses we adopt. Why do you think you embrace the goth lifestyle?"

"I wouldn't know. I'm not goth."

"Ah, but you *are*. It's part of the goth mythology that one is not truly goth until they are not-goth. You've heard the jokes: I'm so goth I'm dead. I'm so goth I died and didn't notice. I'm so goth I'm not-goth? Well, I'm so not-goth I'm goth, and so are you. But lifestyling isn't reality. Reality is money and pain. And pleasure." A monarch flutters down and lands on his arm. He brushes it away. "And butterflies. Butterflies are real too."

"Why did you tell Dylan to give me the chrysalis?"

Draco—I am thinking of him as Draco now—says, "It's my calling card. I wanted to meet you."

"Why?"

"I became intrigued by your on-line persona. You were always the most interesting creature in Transylvania."

"But how did you know who I was?"

"You told me."

"No I didn't."

"Ah, but you *did*. Every time you visited the chat room you revealed yourself. One time you mentioned that Anne Rice was in town signing books, so I knew we lived in the same city. Another time you mentioned walking to Crosstown Center, so I knew which school district you lived in. You've said things about how you dress. I even knew that you had diabetes, based on some of our chats about blood—who but a diabetic would use words like 'hypoglycemic' or 'blood glucose'? You let on far more than you knew. It was a simple matter for me to deduce that you were a student at Seward High. All I had to do then was ask young

Dilly to identify you. It was not difficult for him to pick you out of the student body. How many highly intelligent diabetic goths could there be in one high school?"

"What is he, your secret agent?"

"He does favors for me."

I think that I should be frightened, but for some reason I'm not. His voice sounds so reasonable, and he seems to appreciate me for my mind. It's not as if he's some demonic fiend lusting after my tender young body. It's a little strange that he would go to all that trouble to find me, but maybe he's just a lonely, pathetic middle-age man who likes to play vampire. I don't really think he's going to *do* anything. Not here. Not with all these people in the next room.

Draco says, "In any case, I apologize for not being more direct with you. I just wanted to meet you without . . . well, I feared that Draco's on-line reputation might frighten you. I wanted you to meet Just Plain Wayne."

"It's not like I ever really thought you drank pig's blood," I say.

"You never know." He refills my wine-glass from the bottle of port. I don't remember drinking the first glass. "Sometime I'd like to talk with you about your theory concerning the origins of vampirism. It's a truly remarkable piece of deduction. The idea of diabetes and vampire legends being linked—the first time you mentioned it in the chat room, I thought you might be a university professor. How did you come up with it?"

"You mean about diabetics being the first vampires?"

Draco nods, and I start talking. I tell him about finding the sick bat when I was six years old, and about the rabies shots, and about how I later read descriptions of untreated diabetes. Then somehow I got onto the topic of how everybody who ever got saved by technology is technically Undead.

"Then I must be Undead too," he says.

"What happened?"

"I was in a car accident. If not for the airbag I would've been killed."

"That doesn't count. The car is technology. If technology kills you *and* saves you, they cancel each other out."

Draco laughs, and I laugh too. Beneath the white foundation makeup, smeared lipstick, and leather corset is someone I can talk to.

I am not a fool. I know that Draco is no supernatural creature. He is just a man, old enough to be my father, who has never grown up. So what? Where does it say you have to grow up? Do rock stars ever grow up? What about old men who spend hours every week playing with model trains? Why is being a pretend vampire any weirder than a doctor who pretends to care about his patients, or a diabetic pretending to be normal? Or going to church and pretending to believe in God? People do these things all the time.

Although Draco has never really grown up, he is not a boy. Nor is he a parent, a teacher, a doctor, or a shrink. He knows what it means to be different, to stand outside the safe, confining bubble of mundane existence. He is not afraid to be not-goth. He doesn't treat me like a child. He gives me port wine. Words flow between us, megabytes of understanding, and when he is making an important point his hand touches my knee and he looks fearlessly into my eyes.

We talk for what seems like hours. The port wine has settled my stomach. Maybe it is the alcohol, or some other magical property. Every now and then someone enters the greenhouse with a question, or just to say hello or good night or thank you. I am the Queen of the Damned, sitting beside Draconius the Vampire King as he deals with his subjects. One very drunk girl comes in to ask him if she can sleep in the spare bedroom.

"Of course, my dear," says Draconius the Vampire King. The girl stumbles off, and he turns back to his Queen. "You are also welcome to stay here. Anytime you want to, anytime you need a place to stay." His hand is back on my knee, only this time it doesn't leave. "You are family now."

For a few long seconds I fall into the fantasy. I don't have to go home. I don't have to go to school. I can stay here forever, raising butterflies and . . . I look down at his hand. When was the last time anyone touched me? I think it was Vice-principal Gruber's meaty paws. Draco's hand is smaller. It feels hot on my knee. And heavier.

"Would you like to stay here with me tonight?" he asks.

I look down at his hand. Its back is thick with cracking foundation makeup. The nails at the end of his stubby fingers are short and ragged, chewed to the quick. I swallow, and suddenly the nausea is back.

"I'd better not." I can't take my eyes off his hand. A hollow, panicky feeling fills my chest.

"I have to go now," I say.

"Why? You're not afraid of me, are you?"

"No." I'm not afraid of him, but I'm afraid

of something. "I just have to go." But I don't move.

Draco is giving me a searching look. He says, "Do you know what I would like?"

"No."

"I would like you to have dinner with me. Would you have dinner with me? Here?"

"Right now?" My stomach rolls.

He smiles. "No, not now. A week from today. Are you free?"

Free? I've never been free, I think. I've been trapped my whole life, and now it is his thick fingers on my knee holding me motionless. "What day is that? Friday?"

"Friday, yes."

"Just you and me?"

"Does that frighten you?"

"No," I say. But it does.

"Will you come?"

"I'm a vegetarian."

"A vegetarian vampire?" He laughs and I see his stumpy little teeth stained with red lipstick and port, and white foundation cracking at the corners of his mouth, and beads of sweat gathering at his hairline. His hand shifts, his fingers wriggle like fat white grubs on my thigh. The muscles in my legs flex and suddenly I am standing. Blood rushes from my head; I drop my wineglass and stagger to the side. Broken glass crunches beneath my heel. Draco grabs my elbow, steadying me.

"Are you okay?" His voice sounds far away.

The room is spinning. "I'm fine," I hear myself say.

"Sit," he says, tugging at me.

I pull my arm away. The spinning slows; the room shudders back into focus. "I have to go," I say. Rubber legs carry me off as a woozy thought drifts across my brain: So this is what it feels like to be drunk.

Draco calls after me, "Lucinda!"

I push through the plastic curtain. The party is still going strong. Weevil has organized an apple-bobbing competition. The kitchen is full of grinning, apple-eating wet-heads. Their voices are the roaring of a waterfall and their faces are cartoons. I blink and afterimages appear on the walls. My legs seem to have grown another six inches. Is it the wine, or am I having an insulin reaction?

I blink again and find myself in the library. I don't remember leaving the kitchen. I stare at the shelves, the titles all running together: *Exsanguinarius Rex The Practical Vampyre Book of Black Magic & Ceremonial Magic Pictorial Key to the Tarot Cream of the Jest. . . .*

Maybe I *am* having an insulin reaction. I rubberleg my way to the next room and find a bowl of Halloween candy on an endtable. Butterfingers and candy corn and miniature chocolate bars. I grab a handful of the chocolate bars and start eating them one after another. Chocolate coats my mouth; I swallow and imagine a long brown syrupy rope flowing down into my stomach. Chocolate is my favorite way to treat an insulin reaction.

Fiona appears in front of me. Where did she come from? "I thought *you* couldn't *eat* chocolate," she says.

"I can eat anything I want," I say as I shove another bar into my mouth.

"Are you *okay*?"

"I'm fine," I lie. I lurch off. I can't remember how many glasses of wine I had. Everything is confusing. My gut hurts. Too much chocolate? I wander through three or four rooms and suddenly I am facing Fiona again.

"Are you *sure* you're okay?" she asks.

"I've been here before," I say.

She laughs. "Are you *drunk*?"

Maybe I am. My stomach has broken free and is doing backstrokes in my gut. Is it okay to go swimming if you are a full stomach? One part of me laughs at my silent joke while another part tells me that it is time to go.

"Have you seen Dilly?" I ask.

"*Dilly?* You mean *Dylan*? I think he's watching the *fish*." She points to the next room.

I find Dylan sitting before a large aquarium staring at brightly colored tropical fish.

"Hey," I say.

He looks up at me with a silly Dilly grin. "Hi, Lucy!"

"I want to go."

"Now?"

"I want to go now."

He stands up, staggers to the side, and falls flat on his face.

"Oops." He pushes himself up. His nose is bleeding.

"You're drunk," I say.

"I'm okay," he mumbles, touching his nose, looking at the red smear on his hand.

Maybe I'm drunk too, but I'm not so drunk I'd get in a car with him driving. "Where's the jacket?"

"I don't know. . . ." His eyes are pointing in two different directions.

I plunge from room to room, searching, and finally find Mark's letter jacket draped over the back of a chair. I throw it over my shoulders and I'm heading for the door when Draco materializes before me like a movie vampire.

"Lucy," he says, his hands cupping my shoulders. "Are you sure you're all right?"

"Let *go*." I slap his arms aside.

"Are you angry with me?"

"I have to go." But he is standing in front of the door.

"Then I will miss you." He reaches out with his left hand, very slowly. I watch it coming toward my face. The backs of his fingers brush my lips gently, then he brings his hand to his mouth and kisses it where it touched my lips.

My stomach lurches. He sees the revulsion in my eyes. He smiles.

"I have to go," I say again.

Draco shrugs and steps aside, and I am running down the stairs, I am pushing through glass doors, I am running through the night.

26

Snail

I am thirsty.

The sidewalk is slick and hard and peppered with tiny pellets of ice larger than poppyseeds but smaller than peas. It is like snow, and it is like hail. I will call it snail. My cowboy boots skitter and skid on the ice, but somehow I do not fall. I am walking through the snail, protected by Mark's enormous jacket, ice pellets rattling off the hard leather sleeves.

The streets are empty. It must be three or four in the morning. I wonder how many miles away from home I am. Maybe a taxicab will drive by. My boots crunch, my breath is a cloud of steam, my guts are heavy and sore. Maybe I am pregnant, abducted by aliens and seeded with a star child. Or Draco planted a demon child inside me when he touched my lips. Or it is cancer, a huge tumor. I'll take the tumor. The street-lamps are haloed and painfully bright.

I walk past a small house sandwiched between two apartment buildings. The lights are on; the curtains are open. A woman sits at a table drinking from a purple mug. Why is she awake? I stop and watch her through the window. She is drinking tea, I think, and reading a book. Maybe she can't sleep. She sips her tea again; I can almost taste it I am so thirsty. What if she looked out the window and saw me standing there? Would she invite me in? Would she offer me a cup of tea? A glass of water? Or would she call the police? As I am thinking this her head turns and points directly at me. She stares blankly for a few seconds, then returns to her book. Did she see me, or was she looking at her own reflection in the glass?

She turns a page and sips her tea. I do not exist. I am not real to this woman. I am not part of her world. I am thirsty and I am invisible.

I continue down the sidewalk, crunching ice pellets with my boots and grateful for the sound. The snail knows I'm real. It is two inches deep on the sidewalk and a slushy mess on the street. I wish I had called a taxi from Wayne's. I wish someone would stop and give me a ride to Mark's so I could return his letter jacket. It would be terrible if I didn't. Maybe Mark will give me something to drink. Water, port, snakebite, *anything*.

I once read that if you relax your arms and shoulders and hold your head high you can walk all day without tiring. I am very tired. My neck is tucked between my hunched shoulders. I would pull it in all the way if I could, like a snail. My stomach hurts. I don't think I've walked even three miles, and I have at least that far to go.

The twenty-four-hour Laundromat is so bright it stings my eyeballs. Nobody is there, but two dryers are running. The phone is broken. I feed a dollar into the soda machine. Diet or regular? I buy a regular Coke. I need the sugar, I think. I still have a long walk ahead of me. I stand and watch my reflection in the tumbling dryers and drink the Coca-Cola. I am almost done with it when I remember Draco's hand touching my lips and suddenly my belly clenches. I drop to my hands and knees and vomit wine and chocolate and Coke onto the floor. Chaos, upheaval, revelation. The pain is excruciating and the room is whirling. I am being spun and squeezed by a giant invisible gorilla, emptied like a tube of toothpaste.

I've had my last drink ever, I tell myself, and I throw up again.

I hear someone whimpering. It's me.

I am lying on a Laundromat floor staring at a lake of vomit. Disgusting, repugnant, loathsome, repulsive. I climb to my feet. Vomit is soaking onto the leather sleeve of Mark's jacket. I rinse it off in the sink. Maybe it will be okay. I dry the sleeve with a T-shirt someone has left on the folding table and stumble out of the Laundromat. The snail is piled deeper. I slog onward at snail speed.

I am eating snail. It is crunchy and cold and it soothes my throat. I am able to eat three handfuls before the invisible gorilla comes to squeeze a few more ounces of vomit from my aching gut. My brain is not working. There is something I should know; something I should be doing. I am so close. I try to stand up again but my body weighs a thousand pounds. I flop onto my back on the cold wet ground and stare up into the falling snail. *Polyphagia, polydipsia, polyuria, mental obtundation. Abdominal tenderness, decreased bowel sounds. Hypothermia is the rule. . . .* It is not a voice, but a memory. Words I have read.

Polyphagia: uncontrolled eating. Polydipsia: uncontrolled drinking. *Polyhemodipsia*: uncontrolled drinking of blood. Now I am making up words. *Polyhemosnaildipsia*: uncontrolled drinking of bloody snail. Must be that mental obtundation.

I am too thirsty to think and too tired to move. I close my eyes and let the images come, butterflies, vampires, port wine, chocolate. I see a page covered with type. *Polyphagia, polydipsia, poly* . . . I remember now. They are symptoms of the Big Scary: diabetic ketoacidosis. I'm not drunk, I'm dying. My body doesn't need chocolate or Coke, it needs insulin. Did I take my morning shot? Apparently not.

My name is Lucy Szabo. I live at 429 Johnson Avenue. My telephone number is . . . I can't remember. There are so many things I don't know. The last two days are a dream. This is not the twenty-first century, it is two hundred years ago. Transylvania. I can hear the wolves howling. The peasants will find me here in the bright cold morning, my eyes frozen, my oversweetened body covered with snail. I will have become something different. Tomorrow, perhaps, I will rise from my coffin and demand their blood.

I open my mouth and let the tiny pellets of ice fall between my lips.

27

Logic

I see faces.

I see Draco; I see Wayne. I see Guy. I see Mark. I see Fish and Buttface and Dr. Rick. I see a woman drinking tea in the middle of the night. I see myself reflected in the hot glass of a tumbling dryer. I see my mother in the framed photo of herself she keeps on her vanity: beautiful, tall, healthy, cheerful, normal. I see my father—never a handsome man, but always brimming with confidence—now fearful and confused. They are all looking at me.

None of them are real. My eyes are closed, so how can they be real? What did Draco say? Reality is money and pain. And pleasure. But he is wrong. I know he is wrong. Money is a symbol. Pain is a sign or something else. Pleasure is an illusion. So what is real? Butterflies?

Reality is the beeping I hear. And the smell of disinfectant and flowers. And the warm, dry, scratchy fabric.

I hear my mother's voice. "Sweetheart? Honey?" That is real too.

I know where I am now. That doesn't stop my mouth from asking, "Where?"

"You're in the hospital, Sweetie."

Undead again. I open my eyes. She is peering at me. The flesh under her eyes is dark and soft, the smile lines sag on her cheeks, and her skin looks thin and brittle. She looks *old*. When did she get *old*? How long have I been asleep? I want to ask her what year it is, but I am afraid.

"How are you feeling?"

"Tired." I look down my arm at the IV drip. I look down my legs at two balls of white bandage. I wiggle my toes; the bandages move, but it *hurts*. "What happened to my feet?"

"A little frostbite, Sport." My father's voice. He is standing at the foot of the bed. He looks old too. "Your blood sugar was over eight hundred when they brought you in."

"Oh." A new record.

"You were lying in the snow for hours."

I remember that. It was cold. I was thirsty.

My mother says, "We didn't even know you were gone, Honey. I went to your room to wake you up and"—her face crumples and her eyes tear up—"you weren't *there*."

I look away. My eyes land on blue denim legs. I follow the legs up to an orange sweatshirt, to Mark Murphy's freckled face.

"Hey, Skeeter," he says. He doesn't look any older.

"Hi." I don't feel like calling him Monkey Boy.

"Mark found you," my mother says.

"You were curled up under the lilac bushes in my backyard, covered with snow," Mark says. "I thought you were dead."

"So what did you do? Go back inside and eat breakfast?" I mean it as a joke, but it doesn't come out funny. "Just kidding," I say.

He barely smiles. "I brought you inside and called 911."

My father says, "I'll let the doctors know you're awake." He walks out of the room.

"Are you hungry, Sweetie?" my mother asks. I want to reach out and smooth her brow, but I know she'd pull back.

"I'm a little thirsty," I say. She pours a glass of water from the pitcher on the bedside table and offers it to me. The water tastes flat and stale. "Could I get some Diet Sprite or something?"

"I could get one from the machine." She grabs change from her purse and heads out on a Sprite hunt. Good. I need to talk to Mark.

"How long have I been here?" I ask him.

"Since yesterday morning."

"Is that all? My mom looks so *old*."

"She's pretty beat. I don't think she's been home since they brought you here."

"I'm sorry about your jacket. I puked on the sleeve."

He shrugs. "You were sick."

"I was trying to return it to you. I think that's why I ended up in your yard. I guess I wasn't thinking so good."

"I kind of figured that."

"Thanks for not asking."

"Asking what?"

"You know. Where I was and stuff."

Mark shrugs.

"And for not being scared of me."

"I'm a little scared of you," he says.

"But not like you avoid me."

"Why would I do that?"

"You still like me?"

"Like you?"

"Me." I point at myself. "Who I am."

❧

"Ms. Szabo?"

"Hey, Fish."

"Having a bad week?"

"I've had better."

He flips through my chart, shakes his head, then sits down in the chair next to my bed and crosses his legs. "What happened?"

"I was a bad girl."

He raises his eyebrows and waits for more.

"I think I forgot my morning insulin."

"Weren't you testing?"

"I guess not."

"Is that all? Ketoacidosis doesn't usually come on so quickly."

"Well, I'd had a few bad days. I thought I was just, you know, stressed out. Things got kind of out of control. And then I, ah . . . is this just between us?"

Fish thinks about that for a few seconds, then nods.

I tell him as much as I think he can handle. I tell him about the port wine and the chocolate. And when I'm done talking, he tells me that my heart stopped beating for almost two minutes.

"I was dead?"

"Near enough. You got here just in time. Fortunately, you're young and otherwise healthy. The remarkable thing is, Lucy, that you have recovered so quickly. But we're going to have to keep an eye on you for the next few weeks to make sure you haven't suffered any organ damage. And I'd like to schedule you with a diabetes educator to go over your regimen."

"I know what I'm supposed to do. I just didn't do it."

Fish smiles. "That's what they all say."

They let me go home later that afternoon. My mother is into her cheerful act; my father grips the steering wheel with his big hands, saying nothing. I can feel, taste, and smell their fear and anger. I am bad. I have inconvenienced them. Made them worry. Bad girl. Do I feel bad?

Mostly I feel angry. If they hadn't taken away my computer none of this would have happened. I know that doesn't make sense, but I believe it. If they hadn't made me go to school I'd never have punched Gruber in the eye. That doesn't make any sense either. I don't care. I am beyond logic.

I look at the back of my mother's head, at her practical haircut with its streaks of gray. Every one of those gray hairs is my fault, I suppose—although it's really *her* fault for giving birth to me.

It's Dylan's fault too. He got too drunk to drive and so I had to walk home. I am very angry at Dylan. I am even a little bit mad at Mark, and I don't know why. Yes I do. He lent me his jacket. Why did he do that? Why didn't he just say no, or make me tell him why I wanted to borrow it? Why would he just do what I say? He says he's a little scared of me. Why is he afraid?

That's the thing about Draco. He's not afraid of me at all. I can be who I am. Everybody else I know treats me like nitroglycerin. I treat myself that way sometimes. Sometimes I think I'm the worst one of all.

When we get home I shuffle up the stairs in my hospital booties. I won't be able to wear regular shoes for a few days. My room feels small and deserted. The crumpled shell of the chrysalis still hangs from the edge of the shelf, my bed is unmade, my clothes are strewn. This is what my mother saw when she went to look for me Saturday morning. I sit at my desk and test my blood sugar. It is perfectly normal—just like everybody else. I could eat something if I was hungry. Or eat nothing at all. For this moment it is as though I do not have diabetes. Perfectly normal.

I sit on the edge of my bed and take off my paper booties and unwrap the gauze bandages and look down at my angry red toes and I start to cry.

Dying has a curious effect on a person. I recommend it to anyone who thinks that they need more insight about themselves. But don't expect to get any happier. When it comes to self-realization, the more you know the less you like. At least that's how it worked for me. I have tremendous insight, but I am miserable.

Insight number one: I could be dead. I am staring up at Rubber Bat, and I could be dead. My toes are throbbing, but I could be dead. My parents are watching TV . . . I could be dead. Instead I am Undead again. Does one cancel out the other, or am I double-Undead? Nobody said that insights have to be logical. I am alive, but I am Undead.

Insight number two: When you are dying, your life does not flash before your eyes. At least mine didn't. That means that I have to pay attention to everything that happens to me from now on, because I only get to see it once. Several interesting things have happened to me lately. I will try to remember them.

Insight number three: When you die and then come back, the people who are there when you wake up are the people who love you.

And that is why I am miserable. Because they are the people I hurt the most.

28

Me

It is four days before I can wear regular shoes again. Four days of shuffling around the house in paper booties, then in a pair of my father's slippers after the booties fall apart. Mostly I don't care what people think, but I would die if anybody saw me in those blue booties.

By Thursday I am able to pull my boots on. I dress in the blackest clothes I have. I slather on the eyeliner and apply a slash of lipstick the color of eggplant. Still feeling naked, I put on my big shades. Then I comb my hair forward over my face. Now I can't see. I push it back and glare at myself.

"Who do you think you are?" I ask.

❦

At school they are all terrified of me. I don't blame them. Who wants to be around someone who could keel over and die at any moment? Why should they waste a precious moment on a surly black-leather goth/not-goth freak when they could be laughing and smiling and having fun with their perky-healthy friends?

In French class, Dylan offers up a tentative smile. I give him the invisible treatment. Sandy Steiner, Little Miss Perfect Diabetic, approaches me in the hall between classes. She asks me how I'm doing.

"Fine," I say. "Why?"

"Well, I heard you had"—she lowers her voice—"*ketoacidosis*!"

"No biggie. A little intravenous insulin and I'm back to normal. You should try it."

"No!" She can't handle it. The very idea of blood sugars over 400 send her into a complete panic.

"You get used to it after a while," I say as I walk away. Of course, it's not true. You never get used to being Undead. But I like messing with Sandy's perfect little brain.

I walk past Gruber and Buttface, talking in the hall. Probably talking about me. Buttface says something but I ignore her. I see Mark coming down the hall, but I don't want to embarrass him by engaging him in public conversation, so I turn away before he spots me.

I trudge through the day. After my last class I am heading for the door when Marquissa catches up to me.

"Hear you had a scary Halloween," she says.

"It wasn't so bad."

"I rode home with Dylan. That was *really* scary. He was so drunk."

"You're lucky you're not dead."

"I hear *he's* got a *thing* for you," Marquissa says, smirking.

"Dylan?"

"No. Wayne," Marquissa says, showing her teeth. How can a smile be so nasty?

Fiona comes up looking very stripy in candy cane socks and a jacket made out of some sort of crinkly gold plastic. "*Who's* got a thing for *who*?" she says, inserting herself into the conversation.

"Lucy's got a boyfriend old enough to be her dad," Marquissa says.

"He is *not* my boyfriend," I say.

"Who?" Fiona asks.

"Weird Wayne," Marquissa says.

"That *guy*?" Fiona looks horrified. *"Really?"*

"You guys are sick." I roll my eyes and walk away.

❦

"So," says Dr. Rick, "how is the plan coming along?"

"Plan?"

"Yes. Your strategy for getting your computer back?"

"Oh. That plan." I laugh.

"Is something *wrong*?" he asks, eyebrows bobbing in eager anticipation. I guess nobody told him about my stroll in the snail.

"No, no, everything is fine," I say. "Actually, I've been making some important decisions."

"Such as?"

"Respect my elders, avoid drugs and alcohol, do my homework, quit smoking, don't hang around with vampires. You know. All the usual stuff."

"I didn't know you smoked."

"I don't."

Dr. Rick is blinking rapidly. "I can't always tell when you're kidding," he says.

"Neither can I."

"I see." He gives me a careful look. "You seem . . . more relaxed today."

"I've had an interesting week."

"Oh? How so?"

I consider telling him everything—it would feel so good to let it all spill out—but the hungry look on his face creeps me out. I realize that he does not truly want me to get my life together. His patients are his entertainment. Dr. Rick is just another vampire, sucking up the twisted energy of his patients.

I decide to load him up with empty calories.

"We're studying acids and bases in chemistry. And reading *The Little Prince* in French class. And I'm rewriting my essay for Mrs. Graham. I've decided to become a personal banker. Personal banking is actually very interesting. Have you ever seen the movie *It's a Wonderful Life*?"

"Of course." He can't hide his disappointment. He wants angst and wickedness, and I'm giving him Jimmy Stewart.

"That's what inspired me to become a personal banker. Either that or a chemist. Did you know that if you mix an acid with a base you get water?"

"How fascinating."

I prattle on about acids and bases and personal banking for another twenty minutes. Dr. Rick, nearly comatose, finally looks at his watch and tells me our time is up.

I am out the door, on my way back to my computerless cell, when my sore toes make a wrong turn and take me toward Harker

Village. Antoinette has nothing new in her window display. Bugs Bunny, bleeding heart, fire-breathing dragon, knives, swords, and chains. Lame, lame, triple lame. How about a big red X on one cheek? Everybody would ask me what it means. I'd glare at them and walk away. Would that make me feel better?

I push through the door and enter the shop. Antoinette is behind the counter, bent over her left foot. At first I think she is clipping her toenails, then I realize that she is tattooing her middle toe.

"Be with you in a sec," she says, not looking up.

"Take your time."

"Is that angry, indecisive Lucy I hear?"

"I'm not angry. I'm pissed off."

Antoinette sets down her tattoo machine, spreads her toes, and admires her work. The first three toes read A-N-T.

"Ant?" I say.

"I'm doing my name. One letter per toe."

"Just in case you forget who you are?"

"Don't laugh, girl. It happens. My mother had Alzheimer's. Doesn't hurt to plan for the future. So what's up with you, kid? Wanna get inked today?"

"I'm thinking of something for my forehead."

"Very painful, but we aim to please. What have you got in mind? Lightning bolt? Scarlet letter? Third eye?"

"How about a window."

"For looking in or out?"

"In. If people could see what I'm thinking then I wouldn't have to explain myself all the time."

She gives me one of her X-ray-eye looks. Antoinette doesn't need a window.

"Could get you in trouble."

"I'm already in trouble."

"What happened?"

"I died."

She stares at me, blinking, and my mouth opens and I gush. I tell her everything. Antoinette is a good listener. She never says a word, her eyes never leave my face, and she has no notebook.

"And now," I say, "I'll probably never get my computer back, and everybody at school thinks I'm a time bomb, and I wish I was somebody else."

Antoinette waits a few seconds to make sure I'm done talking, then says, "So what's the problem?"

"Did you hear anything I said?"

"Yeah. You said you wanted to be somebody else. So what's the problem?"

"My problem is I am who I am."

"No you aren't. Tell me something, when you get up in the morning what do you do? Do you look in the mirror?"

"At some point."

"Why?"

"To see myself."

"Exactly. Every morning you check the mirror to see who you are. And every morning you see somebody new. You don't like what you see? Change. You've done it before. Don't tell me you were born with that scowl. Or that hair. Your roots are starting to show, girl."

"But I'm always the same person inside."

"I sure hope that's not true. Are you the same person today as that stupid little twit who spent Halloween night guzzling port wine with that middle-age cradle-robbing nut-job Wayne Smith?"

"I don't know."

"You see these tattoos?" She thrusts out her thick arms. "Every one of them symbolizes a change in my life, and I've had a lot of change, kid. It's how I keep track. Every tat was for a different Antoinette. Check this out." She points at a red heart on her shoulder with the name Gerry written across it in Old English script. "One of my biggest mistakes. The five months I was with Gerry were heaven and hell on earth, but it's part of who I am."

"What happened to him?"

"He died. I know a lot of dead people. You see this?" She pulls up her top. On either side of her navel are the words *Ride Hard, Die Young*. "That's from my biker days. We tore up every highway from Key West to Anchorage. Those were some wild years. Half the bunch I rode with are dead now. Wouldn't do it again for anything, but I never want to forget it. I was somebody else then. I'm not so interested in dying young anymore."

"Me neither."

"That's good."

"So which one are you now?"

"You mean which tat?" Antoinette smiles and points at her toes. "Today," she says, "I'm Antoinette."

I order a double espresso at the Sacred Bean and find a table in the corner and put my sunglasses on and pretend to be dead again. I turn my mind to stone. Not thinking is hard. I shift gears and try to think about what I'm thinking, but I can't tell the difference between thinking and remembering. Am I having another insulin reaction? I take out my glucose meter and prick my finger and do a test right there at my table. No one is watching; no one cares. A number appears: 112. A good, normal, nondiabetic number.

"Hey, Luce." It's Dylan. He sits down across from me. "How are you doing?"

I shrug.

He tips his head and looks at me. Those blue eyes that once made my heart stutter now look vacant and pale. "Don't you like me anymore?" he asks.

"I liked you better before I knew who you were."

He starts to laugh, then sees I'm not joking.

"Wayne's little errand boy," I say.

"I'm not his errand boy. I just thought you'd, you know, like to meet him. He's a cool guy."

"Wayne? Cool? I don't *think* so."

"I know he's kind of dorky, but he throws a great party."

"Yeah, real great. Getting a bunch of kids drunk."

"So? It beats sitting around the house watching TV."

"Are those your two choices? TV or drinking? I feel sorry for you. You and all your pathetic friends."

He sits there for a few seconds with his brow wrinkled, then shrugs and stands up and walks away.

Suddenly I feel awful. Now I'm being just as judgmental and self-righteous as Dr. Rick. One day I'm guzzling port and hanging out with Butterfly Wayne, and a few days later I'm berating Dylan for doing the same thing.

I catch up with him outside.

"Hey, Dylan."

He turns and gives me a cold look.

"I'm sorry," I say. "I didn't mean that."

"What *did* you mean?"

"I meant . . . I guess I've changed. I'm somebody else now."

He gives me a long, scathing look. "Congratulations," he says, then turns and walks away.

29

Blue Sky

Color stripper is possibly the most noxious substance you can buy without being investigated by the FBI. I'm surprised they sell it to minors. I follow the directions carefully, wearing green plastic gloves and breathing as little as possible. It takes two bottles and almost three hours to do the job.

At one point my mother knocks on the door to tell me I have a phone call. "I'm not home," I yell back.

"What are you *doing* in there?"

"Nothing!" I shout. Then I breathe in a bunch of fumes and start coughing.

I hope I haven't bleached my lungs.

❦

I show up at the dinner table in a towel turban. I am Lucy, I am Sweetblood, I am Swamirama. My father doesn't seem to notice my headgear, but my mother keeps looking at me, curious. Finally she can't stand it anymore. She has to ask.

"Sweetie, did you do something to your hair?" She looks so pathetically anxious that I take pity on her. I stand up and slowly unwind the towel from my head.

My father says, "Good Lord, Sport."

My mother says, "Oh my!"

I run my fingers through my new hair. It's pretty much back to its original cornsilk blond, a color I haven't seen for almost three years. Of course, the stripper turned the hairs stiff as broomstraw, so I had to cut it back a bit. Quite a lot, actually. The fact is, I've got eyebrow hairs that are longer. I am Sinéad O'Connor, I am Captain Picard, I am Charlie Brown.

I sit back down and help myself to some "vegetarian zucchini casserole," a recipe my mother clipped from *Diabetes Forecast* magazine. I eat a few bites—it's not bad—then look up. They are still gaping at me.

"Maybe this would be a good time to show you my tattoo," I say.

My father's eyes protrude and a vein on his forehead pulses visibly. My mother's hands flutter like wounded birds.

"Just kidding," I say quickly. "No tattoos today." I grin to show them I'm joking. My mother's hands settle into her lap, and my father slowly smiles. I wink at him. He winks back.

Saturday arrives bright blue and unseasonably warm. Bizarro weather. The snail has melted. They say it will get up to eighty degrees—a new record high for November. I am sitting on the chaise longue in the backyard with my red toes and my white head soaking up sunlight—the ultimate test for a vampire. So far, I have observed no signs of meltdown.

I am reading my chemistry textbook. Acids and bases. Fascinating stuff. Utterly compelling. They should teach this stuff in kindergarten. A roomful of five-year-olds playing with hydrochloric acid. Hydrogen ions everywhere. The chemistry book is getting heavier. My hands slowly lose their grip and it plops down onto my thighs. The clouds are high and wispy today; I see angels and ghosts. I rise to join them. It's nice up there. I am doing loops around a cirrus cloud when my mother's voice reels me back to Earth.

"You have a phone call, Sweetie." Apparently, telephone privileges have been reinstated. She hands me the phone.

I cover the mouthpiece with my hand. "Who is it?"

"He didn't say." She heads back into the house.

I put the phone to my ear. I hear faint music, and breathing.

After a time, he speaks. "Sweetblood? Are you there?"

I say nothing.

"I missed you at dinner last night," he says.

I set the phone on the grass and return my attention to the clouds. As I rise up past the clouds and into the endless blue sky I can still hear his voice, tinny, distant, and inconsequential.

Scott's Sports Central has one extra-large orange and blue Seward jacket left in stock. I put it on over my black everything—a fashion statement of the utmost variety—and walk over to Mark's. I bang on the back door with my fist. Mark answers the door all groggy with his hair sticking out every which way.

"I wake you up from a nap?" I say.

He nods, his eyes taking in my getup.

"I got you a new jacket." I shrug it off and hold it out. "You'll have to take the letter off your old one and sew it on."

Mark doesn't take the jacket. He is too busy staring at my hair.

"Here." I throw the jacket over his head and walk away.

A few seconds later he comes running after me. "You didn't have to get me a new jacket."

"I didn't want you to walk around with puke stains on your sleeve all year."

"Well . . . thanks."

"You're welcome. Thanks for saving my life."

"No problem. I owed you one."

My boot heels are going *tock tock tock* on the sidewalk. Mark is wearing running shoes, which make a sound like *scrish scrish scrish*. His new jacket is hanging over his right shoulder.

"I don't know why you're wearing that," I say. "It's almost eighty degrees out."

"It's November. Could snow any second."

"*Snail*. It might *snail* anytime." *Tock scrish tock tock scrish tock tock* . . .

"What are you talking about?"

"Nothing. I'm delirious."

"Having more of that keto-whatchacallit?"

"Yes. About to keel over any second now."

"I'll catch you."

"How do you like my hair?"

"Can I touch it?"

"At your own risk, Monkey Boy."

His big hand cups the top of my head and gently wriggles the little hairlets. *Tock tock scrish tock tock scrish . . .*

"That is so cool," he says, lifting his hand away.

"I'm still the same twisted individual. Just different."

"You still Skeeter?"

"Still Skeeter, still Lucy, still Sweetblood, still all of them."

"Good. I like you that way."

"Which way?"

"I like you all those ways."

Scrish tock tock . . . We walk for a wordless while with the autumn sun warm on our backs, and every now and then his arm brushes mine.